Hope Sheffield

Blood
Mother

This is a work of fiction. Names and characters are the product of the author's imagination and any resemblance to actual persons, living or dead, is entirely coincidental.

ISBN 978-0615484334

To Jeff,
our children,
and my parents

Chapter One

Her telephone manner escalating from assertive to hostile, Laura Sumner grabbed a pen from the top of her marble desk as if its point could protect her from retaliation. Behind her swivel chair, a wall of teak shelves neatly lined with leather casebooks provided rear fortifications. Her primary areas of vulnerability were the open door to her right and two small windows facing Lake Michigan. When she became a share partner at Winters & Early three years ago, Laura had traded the grubby west view, rooftops and train tracks and factories, for this pristine expanse of blue. She never looked at it, but she sometimes felt its eyes upon her, blankly staring.

"Look, we'll go to trial on this." Laura gouged her pen into her legal pad. "The costs are not going to intimidate my client, and when we prevail, this case will set an excellent precedent for us. I simply can't justify any compromise. We can stop this thing now and save you further expenses. Otherwise, we'll be ready for trial next week. No, talk to your client and get back to me. If we spend much more attorney time, we might as well just go to trial and be done with it. Yeah. Talk to you soon."

Laura hung up. Her mouth twitched slightly. She was used to bludgeoning people, she had been doing it for years. She worked in a man's world, and she had to act tough to get respect, to get what she wanted for herself and for her clients. But lately her home had become another battlefield, and sometimes she felt she was losing herself, as if her soul had melted away and all that was left was the tough act.

When she had first met Lewis, they were still students at the University of Chicago. Laura had admired Lewis's intellect, and his determination to live up to his ideals. She was a child, they both were, and they lived in a fantasy land. When she started to work, she had to be aggressive and controlling, and it was hard for her to back off, even at home. It was hard, but she might have done it if Lewis had helped her, if he had understood. Instead, he sulked like a spoiled child whose mother wouldn't buy him a Power Ranger. She had lost respect for him then. Thank God for Richard and Marie, she thought. They pierced through to a soft, private place, so that she knew she still had a heart.

Laura shuffled absently through the stack of mail on her desk. She did love Marie. She pictured her daughter, warm with sleep when she arrived home most nights, her small fist clutching the frayed pink blanket that Richard had sent as a baby present. Laura smiled at life's ironic twists, Richard Orwell the legal monolith casually bestowing Marie's most precious gift. Or perhaps it was perfectly fitting. Laura imagined Richard and Marie together, side by side, their soft blonde hair, their mirror blue eyes.

Laura winced. The truth was, Laura simply didn't know which man, Lewis or Richard, was Marie's real father. She remembered that night two years ago, the triumph in a Detroit courtroom after so many months of late nights with their heads drooped over the same document, the bristles of desire shooting between them as her love for Lewis faded and expired. Then too much champagne and the cool cotton hotel sheets and the thrill of Richard's power joined to hers. Later, alone, shocked not so much by her act as its possible results, her carelessness, the chance she had taken, she made sure to engage Lewis, to protect herself from messiness and scandal. Lewis was her dupe, lured to bed to blur the results of her real passion. Although she and Lewis were now divorcing, her personal relationship with Richard must remain secret until after Marie's custody disposition. Legally, if not biologically, Marie was Lewis's child. And Laura knew beyond all doubt that, according to longstanding judicial principles, good mothers did not have love affairs.

It was noon. Laura's stomach twisted, and she was cold, in the Arctic July of the air-conditioned business world. She stood, pulled on her suit jacket and smoothed her skirt. She would just grab a cup of soup from the coffee room for lunch today. She still had to prepare for tomorrow's deposition and Wednesday's motion for summary judgment, and the answer was due in the Granger case on Friday. And she might have to go to trial next week. God, she hoped that case would settle.

"Are you hungry?" Richard Orwell popped his exquisite silver head around the door frame.

"Starving, but I'm too busy. Liquid diet today, I'm afraid."

He entered her office and shut the door. The windows watched unblinking as he came close to Laura and slid his large, fine hands down her sides. Even though he had touched her a thousand times before,

Laura could tell he was still feeling her, still appreciating her fragility and her softness. She stared into his face, his frozen blue eyes, the square jaw and bony nose and swollen lower lip. She felt a tendril of heat blaze up through her body, and she blushed, a deep blood red.

"Then tonight. Come, you must eat some time." His hands clasped her small waist, his thumbs disturbingly pressing her stomach.

"I have to get home tonight to put Marie to bed." She squirmed in his grasp.

"Silly girl, the maid can do that."

"But I want to," she said weakly.

Richard released her. "All right, then. Some other time." He turned to leave.

"No, Richard, wait. Come back. Tonight would be wonderful. I would love to have dinner with you."

"Seven o'clock." He reached out to stroke her cheek, and then he left.

It was only one night, Laura thought. And she might still arrive home in time. Otherwise, she could do it tomorrow. Marie would still be there. Eventually, she would win custody of Marie, it was inevitable. Little girls need their mothers, every judge knows that. Disturbed, but diligent, she obtained her cup of soup and returned to her desk.

Lewis stopped his bicycle at the light at the corner of Sheridan Road and Kenilworth Avenue. He removed his tweed jacket and folded it neatly over the right handlebar. He had overdressed for the summer weather, but he felt that the jacket created the proper tone for an assistant professor, serious but informal, classically academic. It was a brilliant July day, huge oaks shimmering green in the sunlight, the air caressingly warm. Bursts of pink and orange and red, the North Shore summer selection of impatiens, petunias, and geraniums, bordered expansive lawns.

Peddling north on Sheridan Road, Lewis glimpsed Lake Michigan, sparkling and changeable. Some days it lay glassy and serene, others it crashed white foam caps against the sandy shore. In winter its edges froze, creating a weird moonlike setting of solid waves along the beach. When he was a boy, Lewis had wandered on the ice chunks, thrilled with their bizarre appearance and the crisp air and the possibility that he might suddenly crash through into the icy waters below.

He turned left onto Cherry Street. The streets in Winnetka had tree names, Oak and Pine, Cherry and Elm and Maple. Like the trees, the houses were majestic and old, solid and enduring. Fences were painted, flowers planted, and lawns were mowed and edged, though rarely by their owners, who were too busy to perform menial work. In fact, Lewis rarely saw them in their yards at all. He imagined children from Chicago liberated onto these massive lawns, running and playing catch or tag or kick-the-can. Instead, mothers or babysitters drove their children to expensive organized activities. Lewis felt the rigorous chill of this life, but Laura had insisted on it, and, as usual, he had acquiesced. The schools were good, and it was safe here, for Marie.

Lewis steered into the alley and unlocked the garage door. He tried to keep the garage locked most of the time. Last fall, on the night before school started, vandals had entered his neighbors' garage and punctured their tires, and bicycles were stolen regularly. Lewis read occasionally in the local paper about home break-ins through open windows or unlocked back doors, thefts of jewelry or a few hundred dollars, but that had never happened to anyone he knew.

In the backyard, Angelica was pushing Marie on a swing that Lewis had hung from a tree limb. She trotted under the swing as she pushed, sending Marie soaring. Marie giggled recklessly, convinced of her safety and enjoying the feeling of flight. A million years ago, at the graduate school party where they had met, Laura had told Lewis that she had always wished she could fly. He had cherished that image of her, a girl and then a lithe young woman, her head tipped enthusiastically toward the clouds. That was the Laura of long ago, before lawyering had nailed her to the ground. She lived in an eighty-story cave now. She couldn't even see the sky.

"Hello, Angelica. Marie!"

Lewis ran up to his baby girl, his arms widespread. Angelica stepped aside as Lewis began to push the swing, with Marie kicking excitedly.

"So, Angelica, everything all right today?"

"Yes, Mr. Lewis. We went to the park, we took the new big wagon like you said, and Marie had fun in the sandbox. She ate a good lunch, and she just got up from her nap. That Mike, he's been working around outside, scraping the paint . I gave him a tuna sandwich and a coke for lunch. Umm, Mr. Lewis, I'm not feeling so good, and I was wondering, could I go home early?"

"That's fine. Are you well enough to put together some dinner first? My mother is coming over. Nothing fancy, just a little more of whatever you were going to make would be great."

"Yes, I can."

"Great. Thanks." As Angelica retreated toward the house, Lewis noticed a bright red stain bloomed on her shorts like a rose. Female problems. Well, he had them too. He peeked around the corner. Standing on the ladder, Mike seemed to be peering through Marie's bedroom screen. "Hi, Mike," he shouted. "How's it going?"

Mike jerked away, nodded, and resumed scraping the window frame. The telephone rang, and Lewis rushed inside to beat the answering machine.

"Hi. Something came up, and I'm not going to make it home until around nine." Laura's voice penetrated the phone wire like a needle scratching his skin.

"Gee, that's a shock. I don't know what Marie and I are going to do after you've moved out. Things will be so different around here."

"Look, I don't have time for this." The screen door slammed, and Angelica came in with a whimpering Marie. She handed Marie a half-empty juice bottle and sat on a kitchen chair to cuddle her. "I just wanted to ask you, would you please try to keep Marie up until I come home, so that I can give her a bath and spend a few minutes with her. I hope that's not too much to ask. She is my daughter."

"Laura, that's ridiculous. Marie is not some toy you can pick up and throw down whenever you feel like it. If the child is tired, I'm not going to force her to stay awake to gratify some sporadic mothering urge of yours. You can damn well come home at a reasonable hour if you want to see her." Lewis glanced self-consciously at Angelica's huddled back.

"You seem to forget that if you want this child to have a decent house to live in and a college education, somebody around here has to earn a living. Who do you think paid for your last eight years of graduate school? And what sinkhole do you think we'd be crawling into at night on your salary? I am doing the best I can for Marie, and someday she's going to understand that. God, I don't know why I'm defending myself to you."

"Someday. What about now? Money isn't everything, Laura."

"Christ, you give me a pain. Can't you do any better than that after all that education? And does that mean you're going to drop the demand for child support from the divorce petition? Not bloody likely, I'd say. I am keeping you, Mister, and all I ask is that you play with Marie for a few extra minutes so that I can give her a bath. I have another call. I'll see you tonight."

She hung up. Lewis's hands were trembling. This was unbearable. He and Laura had loved each other once, but now the stress of simply talking to her scoured his flesh like sandpaper. He looked at Angelica, earnestly rocking Marie.

"I'll take her while you make dinner. Then you can go home. Sorry about that," he said lamely. He pulled Marie from Angelica's lap and headed to the family room. Marie touched his face and studied him with Laura's frosty blue eyes.

Angelica stood in the kitchen and stared at the hand-painted tile counter, shepherds and hens and weather vanes. Laura had told her to scrub the grout with a toothbrush soaked in bleach. Maybe now that Lewis was home she could run down to the basement to get the supplies. The basement door was bolted shut, and Lewis wouldn't let her open it unless someone was watching Marie. The stairs were steep, and he didn't want any accidents.

She felt a familiar dampness between her legs. She had to tend to herself, and then she had to make dinner. It was too late for the grout, and Laura would be angry. Angelica hurried to the bathroom to change her soaked pad. She cradled its weight and warmth in her hand, then rolled it neatly in a cocoon of toilet paper and placed it in the wastebasket. A tear slid down her round, brown cheek. She reached up and ground it into her skin. It wasn't fair.

Chapter Two

Fifteen years ago, Meredith Bennett had hung a framed poster of "Sunday Afternoon on the Island of La Grande Jatte" on the cement block wall opposite her desk, where the window should have been. Now, at age forty, Meredith might have replaced the popular scene with a numbered print by a trendy River North artist, or at least with a more obscure poster, but she liked looking up from her casebooks and files to see the familiar sunny park. It reminded her of simpler times.

Meredith had always wanted to be a prosecutor. She had grown up in Kansas City, not on the Kansas side with the art museum and the nationally recognized high school, but in a nearly rural section of the Missouri side, where her classmates, male and female, had greeted her determination with ridicule and the label "women's libber." To her dismay, she had since discovered that they had a valid point. Meredith was undeniably a woman, and that created, not the absurd spectacle they had anticipated, but a serious conflict within herself.

Three years into her legal career, at twenty-eight, Meredith had married Dr. Alexander Bennett. She had loved him so much, in fact, that she had taken his name as a symbol of their unity, despite her contrary feminist leanings. Alexander was tall and harrowingly thin, with romantic gray smudges under his eyes from serious sleep deprivation. She had met him in a hospital emergency room, where he tended an ankle she had sprained tripping over a curb. He wrapped the ankle, instructed her in its care, and requested her phone number. Meredith chided him for unprofessional conduct and then happily provided her card. The next week, Alexander treated her to a spaghetti dinner and a movie, during which he slept, his head lolling familiarly on her shoulder.

Later, she wondered if Alexander's status as a doctor had attracted her and then worn thin, or whether he was simply kinder when he was trying to obtain her. She felt that she had truly loved him, and the injury he had inflicted still stung. They had been married ten years and produced two daughters when she realized that all his late nights were not, strictly speaking, medical emergencies. She still could not believe he had divorced her to marry his receptionist. Her high school taunters would certainly get a laugh out of that.

Warming her hands around a styrofoam cup, she stared at the papers on her desk. A woman from northwest Chicago had stolen two skirts and a fake gold chain from J.C. Penney's. Two years ago, during her divorce, the State's Attorney had asked Meredith to work downtown, a regular diet of assaults and rapes and murders, the vision of courtroom excitement that she had cherished throughout her education. But Meredith had declined in order to minimize her commute, her hours, and her degree of preoccupation. Her daughters, she knew, wanted her physical presence and her attention, and as their mother, she needed them to feel happy and secure. As an ambitious young woman, she never would have predicted the reality of her life now, forty and alone, with full responsibility for two preteen daughters, a docket of shoplifting cases, and stale coffee in a disposable cup.

Tossing down the lukewarm dregs, she grimaced and glanced at her watch. It was ten minutes to nine. The new improved Mrs. Alexander Bennett was probably just rousing herself for a quick trip in the Jag to Elizabeth Arden, while Meredith scrabbled her fingers blindly through last month's Supercut. Of course she wasn't jealous of the lovely Shawna. Meredith was a lawyer, a vital cog in the criminal justice system, while Shawna was merely a decoration for Alexander's bed, like a stuffed cat or a lace throw pillow.

She stood, smoothed her navy skirt, picked up her files, and marched across the green carpet out the glass double doors into the cavernous tiled body of the courthouse, and then down the narrow stairway to the lobby. Her heels clicked past corn-rowed women drooping on wooden benches, anxious young men in tee shirts and jeans, and red-faced suits dangling briefcases. Pervading everything was the incongruous reek of popcorn, perked fresh in the lobby newsstand, just like at the movies. Every morning it hit her again, cheap and nauseating. Yet, when she passed the stand to go home at night, she realized she had acclimated to it. She could hardly smell it at all.

Meredith opened the glass door of Courtroom F and passed the rows of scrappy defendants and the counsels' tables brimming with public defenders. She rested her files on the edge of the empty jury box and nodded to the clerk. This was their courtroom. Retail theft, battery, burglary, and resisting the peace.

"All rise. Court is now in session, the honorable Judge Jordan presiding," called the sheriff, a short middle-aged woman in the traditional navy and metal, as the judge assumed his elevated position beneath an enormous Circuit Court of Cook County seal.

The clerk called names. "He's not here. He never shows," Meredith reported, and the judge issued arrest warrants. Some defendants approached alone, looking befuddled. "Do you have a lawyer?" the judge asked. "Do you have a job? Go talk to the public defender and see if you qualify for her services," or, "Talk to the bar lawyer, he'll be here soon." Sheriffs in dark shirts and shiny badges milled in and out. The telephone rang, and a baby started to cry. "Clerk, you just call the cases and be quiet! I thought we'd solved that problem!" the judge bellowed. A victim, a graying, tired man, and a defendant, a teenaged girl, faced the judge, as Meredith explained that it didn't matter that the misdemeanor file was missing, because the crime had been upgraded to a felony. A guy whose name was called forty-five minutes ago sauntered in, and the J.C. Penney crook got probation. The clerk got on the phone to call the bar attorney, who still hadn't arrived, and the judge recessed the court.

"I'm going outside. I need a cigarette bad," the clerk reported to the crowd. Meredith retrod the rubberized stairs to her office.

Perching on the edge of her chair, she picked up her telephone and punched in her voice mail code. "Hi, Meredith? It's Shawna. Yup, well, I was just upstairs in the girls' room, and I found Maggie's hairbrush and that little blanket scrap thingy that Lucy likes to hold when she's sleeping. And I was thinking again, wouldn't it make sense, instead of you always having to come out and pick everything up every time, if they had their own stuff here. I mean, this is their home too, and I'd be glad to take them out shopping, and they could have their own stuff that would just stay here, instead of packing a suitcase every time and forgetting everything one place or the other. So, just think about it, and let me know if you want to come over and pick up their stuff. Thanks. Bye."

Meredith hung up. "This is their home too," she whined to herself, mimicking the girlish tones which apparently hoisted Alexander into a pillar of manhood. She imagined Shawna, who had unabashedly stolen her husband, out shopping with her daughters, Shawna flashing his credit card and wiggling her tight-butted jeans and swinging the Nordstrom shopping bags overflowing with outfits that Meredith could not and would not afford. "But it's our pleasure," Shawna would insist. Shawna was supposed to be the wicked stepmother, but instead she had somehow cast herself as Cinderella's fairy godmother, lavishing the poor stepchildren with gowns and glass slippers. As deeply as Meredith resented Shawna's interference with her daughters, she continued to smile graciously and grit her teeth. Meredith certainly did not want to risk forcing the children to choose between them. She still had the third degree burns from their last competition.

Meredith checked her watch and hurried to the bathroom. She stood doubtfully over the discolored toilet seat and then winced at its plastic chill against her skin, unprotected from alien predators by the toilet paper squares her mother had always insisted she apply. Well, now her mother was in Florida, where bacteria were probably the size of a dinner plate. So, why was it that, at age forty, every damned time Meredith went to a public toilet, her mother was there in the stall with her, telling her how to manage it? She adjusted her clothes, flushed, and stomped defiantly past the sink without washing her hands. She was a busy, important lawyer who had to get back to the courtroom to mete justice to the antisocial.

She entered the courtroom and resumed her post near the judge's dais. The public defenders, chatting quietly, lounged at the counsel tables across the room, while she stood alone, the power of the state, upholding the rule of law for J.C. Penney, who had no crying babies or unfulfilled yearnings or overdue rent. And ninety-nine times out of a hundred, she was only a traffic cop, moving cases to this time next month, when hopefully the miserable would show up on their own, possibly with their lawyers, so that she could make the same deal she made over and over again, which the judge would have made without her.

"Court is back in session. Please remain seated and quiet," announced the sheriff. Meredith straightened up and went back to work.

Chapter Three

Mike eased the ladder away from Marie's window and lowered it to the ground. Touching his nose, he felt small damp beads, a protective fluid his body had produced to heal his skin. He had pulled away from the window screen too roughly when Mr. Sumner caught him straining to see into Marie's bedroom, such a delightful room, pink teddy bears dancing in a pale blue sky. Mike could imagine Marie in her crib at night under that sky, sunny curls surrounding a face shiny clean and relaxing into sleep. It was a heavenly, enticing picture. He had to stop thinking about it.

Mr. Sumner had said that he could leave the ladder in the backyard, but he didn't want Marie to trip on it and hurt herself. He lifted the ladder and started to walk it toward the garage, but it was heavy and awkward, and he was tired, and he stumbled and knocked his leg painfully against the metal sides. Finally he rested it flat behind the swing, beside the hedge between the Sumners and their neighbors. That ought to be fine for tonight. Marie was just a little girl, she probably didn't play outside after dinner. He pictured her in her evening bath, her bright hair streaming, her chubby limbs splashing the water as she played with a rubber duck or a plastic boat. He didn't want to think about that, her white skin pink from the steam, her soft, satin body. Well, she was safe

16

and sound in her sturdy stucco house. He smirked as he thought of the three Sumners, like the Three Little Pigs. Marie was a little piglet, wasn't she? And he was the Big Bad Wolf.

Ambling along the flagstone path, Mike wiped his hands on his blue jeans and gazed up at her window, at the front corner of the house. He remembered the Big Bad Wolf, the way he would shout to the pig inside the house and arrange a meeting for the wee hours of the morning. But the pig always escaped, and the wolf ended up in the soup pot. Just keep walking, he thought, and he did it. He passed her window and then he stepped, a square at a time, along the sidewalk back to his mother's house.

The house was a stiff chocolate-brown second floor over a tan brick first floor, like a mass-produced ice cream cone. Mike kept the yard neat, and his mother had set a pot of geraniums on the front steps, matching the pots of geraniums across the street and next door and on the front stoop of every other house in Winnetka. When he was thirteen, Mike had built a ramp that extended from their top step onto the front walk, so that his father could maneuver his wheelchair in and out. They had left the ramp up for almost a year after he died, and then one day his mother had told him to get rid of it. He hadn't known where to put it, so he had left it in the alley for the garbage men to pick up. He had wondered if that would bother her, seeing it in the trash like that, but she never said anything about it. She hardly mentioned his father at all, as if he'd never had one, as if Mike had just appeared in the back garden one day like an Easter egg.

He unlocked the front door and walked back through the dark heat to the kitchen, where his mother stirred a pot of soup, her witch's cauldron. She was thin and blonde, her hair curved in at the bottom and stiff, like a sheet of frozen rain. She wore a red plaid skirt and a white blouse pinned at the throat with a cameo. A coating of sweat glistened through her beige makeup as she patiently cooked Mike's supper.

Mike hated vegetable soup, and his mother knew it. But she insisted that it was economical and nutritious, and she had always made it, even though his dad was a doctor and earned good money. Once, when he was a kid, he had refused to eat it, and she had pushed him to the floor and kneeled on his shoulders and forced the spoon between his teeth, the soup dribbling down the sides of his face and into his ears. His mother had said it was hard to raise a boy virtually alone, with a husband off until all hours doing Lord knew what. He had wished the neighbors could see her, prim and proper Carolyn Ramsey, kneeling on his shoulders and pouring soup down his face. He didn't bother to protest anymore. He just choked it down.

"Hi, Son. Everything go all right today?"

"Sure."

"Supper will be ready soon. Go on upstairs and clean yourself up. I hope they're paying you enough. They're probably fixing it up to sell. Heaven knows, it could use a little work."

Mike looked at his mother. "Why would they sell?"

"Just things I've heard." She shook her head. "That poor little girl. I just don't know what will become of her. Divorce is so hard on children, but parents don't think about that anymore, do they? People can convince themselves of almost anything, just so they end up doing what they want. Scrapping over that baby, and then who takes care of her anyway?"

"Babysitter, mostly."

"Babysitter. Exactly. And they'll probably fire her too, to ice the cake. Go on up and wash, Son. We'll eat when you're ready."

Mike went upstairs to his room. Since they lived near the lake, they didn't have air conditioning, they didn't usually need it, but Mike was sticky, and his arms were coated with paint flecks. So, he thought, the Sumners were going to get divorced and move, and they were using him to get ready. They were using him to take Marie away. He took his tape recorder into the bathroom, set it on the back of the toilet, and shut the door. He stripped off his tee shirt and pants, and he turned the shower on cool.

Mike had spent his senior year of high school in juvenile detention. His mother had told the neighbors that he didn't like New Trier, so they had sent him to Exeter. Mike smirked. She was gutsy, he had to give her credit for that. Since he was still sixteen and a juvenile, the authorities couldn't release his name, and since he had done it in Chicago, the whole incident hadn't even made the papers. Compared to a lot of things that go on in the city, it was not a big deal.

At first, after he came home from detention, he had watched a lot of T.V. He didn't know what to do with himself, and it took his mind off things. One day, he was just flipping around, and he found a talk show host interviewing a guy who had, well, fiddled with his niece. The guy sat in a shadow with colored squares flashing where his head should have been. Mike thought it was cool, the shifting head, his voice thick and far away, as if he were an alien in a space movie. The guy seemed very nice and reasonable. He explained that he still had bad impulses, but now, instead of acting on them, he talked them through with his tape recorder. He would describe his fantasies in detail into the tape, and then he felt better. It was like keeping a journal, except since he wasn't much of a writer, he just talked. Because the guy was a decent person, trying to reform. He didn't want to go to jail. He didn't even like having his face scrambled, but he wanted to keep his job, and he had thought that maybe he could help someone else.

Mike reached out from the stream of water and pushed the red button on his tape recorder. "It's July 19, 1995. Today I saw this little girl, Marie."

After about five minutes, Mike stopped talking. Then he soaped his hair and his beard and his chest and his arms and his legs, and the cool water washed away the sweat and the grime and everything else. He took a washcloth and he scrubbed his armpits and his groin and the soles of his feet. He turned the water hot, to kill all the germs, and then cold, to pre-chill himself for the steamy house. He stepped out of the shower and wrapped his hips in a pink towel. Dripping, he carried the tape recorder back to his bedroom, popped out the tape, and wrote "7/19/95" on its label. He placed it in his dresser drawer with the others.

Chapter Four

"So. Ummm. Well." Meredith had noticed that, at age ten, Maggie frequently felt the need to dominate the dinner conversation, even when she had nothing to say. She would continue to emit low, guttural noises until her brain, thumbing through its rolodex of camp curiosities, finally plucked one worth reporting to what was admittedly a tough crowd.

Lucy stabbed a small bite of chicken with her fork, examined it, and then, glancing covertly at her mother, scraped it off the tines and back onto her plate.

"Everything okay, Luce?" Meredith inquired, distributing carrot sticks from the untouched saucer in the center of the table to her children's plates, so that she could feel she had made an appropriate maternal effort before flinging them into the garbage disposal.

"Yeah. Just a little sauce got on there." A normal eight year- old, Lucy would not taste any condiment containing less than eighty percent sugar and twenty percent chocolate, nor did she approve of foods touching each other.

"Oh. So, Mom. In camp today, Brian Schernoff drowned."

"Really. What happened?" Meredith always tried to take such information in stride.

"Well, we were out paddling around in those little rubber boaty type things --"

"You went to the beach today?"

"Yeah, and Brian kind of like, tipped over, and he was like, going down or something, I mean, I didn't see it or anything, but the counselors had to come over in that red boat thing and pull him out, and he was coughing and everything."

"So he didn't drown. He almost drowned."

"Yeah, well. Whatever."

"Do you wear life jackets in the water when you go out in those boats?"

"Yeah, sure." Dismissively, Maggie reached for the barbecue sauce.

Meredith knew that, if she had been a really good mother, she would have investigated the Skokie Park District's water safety procedures before she permitted her daughters to attend their camp, instead of cross-examining her child after the first reported casualty. She glanced over at Lucy, who had successfully maneuvered her entire meal to adjacent quadrants of her plate.

"Is everybody done?" Lucy asked hopefully.

"No, Honey. Look, Maggie's still chewing. So, did you go to the beach today too?"

"Yes, and it was so boring. Do I have to go to camp? I'm so tired."

Lucy did have a long day, and it probably was tedious and exhausting. Meredith dropped the children at Early Bird Camp on her way to work, followed by Junior Day Camp, and she picked them up from After Camp Fun at a quarter to five. It was a long, hot, structured day for Maggie and Lucy, but it was as short a work day as any full-time lawyer could manage. It was the best she could do, but it was a compromise, and as a result, it was a pain in the butt for everyone.

"Jennifer only goes to camp in the morning, and then her mom takes her home for lunch," Maggie reported in her typical rapier-like manner.

"Well, Jennifer is a lucky girl," Meredith swallowed, proud of her composure. "I'm sorry camp is too long," she continued sincerely, peering into Lucy's shadowy brown eyes. "But I have to work so that we have enough money to buy things we need."

"Why can't Daddy do that?"

"Daddy helps. And also, I need to do something too. A lot of the time, you guys are busy at school or with friends. I don't want to just sit around waiting for you to come home."

Lucy's eyes glazed over. "Is everybody done yet?"

"You could be a teacher," Maggie suggested. "Then you'd get the summer off."

The phone rang, and Maggie leaped up. "Yeah, hi. Oh, yeah, that sounds real good. I'll ask Mom." Maggie muffled the receiver against her flat chest. "Shawna wants to know if she can pick us up from camp at noon tomorrow and take us out for lunch at Neiman-Marcus and then shopping at Northbrook Court. Oh, please, Mom, can we? They have those neat popovers and those little teeny chicken soups, and the mall is so good and cold."

"At noon? Is that your lunchtime? How will that work out?"

"It'll be perfect, don't worry. We just need a note from you, so that they know Shawna's not some kidnapper."

Yeah, Meredith thought. Shawna ought to write Meredith a note. She looked down at Lucy, whose eyes were now riveted pleadingly upon her, and she realized the power she wielded over her children, who were waiting breathlessly for the monosyllabic response on which their future happiness depended.

"Yes, you may go. And tell Shawna thank you."

"Thanks, Mom."

Lucy ran up to her mother and threw her arms around her. They were such dear children, and really, it took so little to please them. Surely they were worth every sacrifice she made.

"Shawna's so cool," Maggie said, returning to her seat.

"I'm sure she is. I think we're done here," sighed Meredith. "Let's clear up."

After she finished the dishes, Meredith set up the sprinkler in the backyard. Maggie and Lucy yanked off their shorts and emerged in their still-sandy bathing suits and began to cartwheel through the spray. Meredith retrieved this morning's newspaper and her glass of iced tea and plopped onto a lawn chair. Strategically positioning herself near the leak in the hose, she sank her feet into a spongy wet spot and turned the pages of the "Chicagoland" section until she hit the headline, "Legal Eagle Superwoman Soars Over Competition," beside the photograph of an attractive dark-haired woman with a savvy half-smile.

When this reporter caught up with Laura Sumner, recently named 1995's "Attorney of the Nineties," she was racing down the stairs from the fiftieth floor of Winters & Early, her prestigious Chicago law firm.

After arguing a multi-state class action before the Seventh Circuit and settling a two billion dollar lawsuit, Ms. Sumner was on her way to her comfortable Winnetka home to read nursery rhymes to her daughter and grab her bag for the red-eye to Washington. On a typical day, she bills fourteen hours, climbs the rock wall at her athletic club, mentors underprivileged inner city youth, and bakes three dozen cookies.

Despite her extensive accomplishments, Sumner describes herself as a normal woman in a two-career family. She resides in a fashionable Colonial in posh Winnetka with her infant daughter Marie and her husband, a sociology professor at Northwestern.

This dedicated superwoman attributes her accolades to native ability, guts, and hard work. "I like being the best," she says simply, but she immediately adds that she also takes her commitment to her daughter very seriously. "I think that, in these troubled times, it is essential for girls to have positive role models," she opines, hurling herself into a cab. "Anybody can wipe up a baby's drool. But how many kids can say, 'My mother just won a multimillion dollar case?' I expect my daughter to be able to say that, in English and in Spanish."

Meredith shut the paper and threw it on top of the hose leak. She would not let this bother her. This woman probably had athlete's foot, a non-existent sex drive, and a thirty percent chance of recognizing her daughter in a line-up. There were no super people, only harried mortals, and something had to give.

Leaning against the back of her chair, she watched her daughters play. They seemed happy, relaxed, and disturbingly oblivious to her presence. She'd fed them dinner and then set up the sprinkler so that they would leave her alone. Any babysitter could do what she'd done this evening, and the chicken would probably have been crispier. Meredith could be off snaring murderers and trying death-penalty cases and getting her picture in the paper, and it wouldn't make a hill of beans of difference to her daughters, who would still be running through the sprinkler a hair's breadth from slamming into each other.

But it must make a difference. She was their mother sitting here, she was with them, projecting vibrations of love and security. And I have chosen them, she thought, I want to be with them. That must matter, and she would not let Laura Sumner and her macho fan club take that away from her. Otherwise, she had blown it big time.

Meredith slumped into the house to get some towels. She trailed across the linoleum floor in the kitchen, past the dishwasher slosh and the knotty pine cabinets and the small formica table and three lonely chairs, through the gold shag living room carpeting, and into the tiny bedroom area, three dry-walled cubbies and an avocado bathroom. Yet, in spite of these sixties horrors and the come-down of it all, she normally didn't miss her old North Shore house that much. Sure it was roomy and actually attractive, but the old steam heat never quite reached the bedrooms, and even when the whole family was home, they were always so far apart. Here it was cozy, like two sweaty arms in an ugly sweater wrapped snuggly around them all. She yanked two pink towels off the linen closet shelf. What she really missed, she thought, was the first apartment she had shared with Alexander after they were married. It was on the third floor of an old house owned by a priest's skittish younger brother who demanded to see their marriage license before he would rent to them. The ceilings slanted, the pipes clanged, and there was no shower, only a footed tub with a rubber hose. But they had loved it. And they had loved each other. She walked outside.

"All right, girls, time to come in and get ready for bed.

Throwing the towels over her daughters' shoulders, Meredith felt momentarily competent. She had anticipated her children's needs and met them, and she was helping them prepare for tomorrow. She shut off the sprinkler as Maggie and Lucy hustled into the house, dribbling water in a slippery trail. A few minutes later, they reappeared, ready for bed.

"Goodnight, Mom."

Maggie presented her face for the requisite kiss and a limp hug. She was getting bigger, and more aloof. Perhaps she felt she was too old to exhibit unrestrained affection for her mother, or perhaps she now saw her mother's flaws and responded accordingly. Deliberately, Meredith squeezed Maggie tight.

"Night, Sweetie. See you in the morning."

"Can you tuck me in, Mom?" asked Lucy, next in line.

"Of course, Sweetie." Meredith followed her into her pastel den and tugged the covers down to the bottom of the bed. "Think just a sheet tonight?"

"Yeah. And I want the fan on high."

Meredith leaned over and hugged her little girl, whose soft, small arms encircled her neck and pulled her close. She breathed in Lucy's warm, powdery smell and felt her smooth against her cheek.

"I don't ever want to let you go," Lucy said.

Meredith sat on the edge of the bed and they stayed for a while together, embracing, feeling the comfort of each other's closeness. Finally, Lucy released her.

"Goodnight," she said, and puckered her mouth to be kissed.

"Goodnight, Honey. See you in the morning." As Meredith lingered in the doorway, she could feel the string between them tugging, pulling on her heart. She turned and glanced at Lucy, who waved. She was wearing one of Alexander's old University of Chicago tee shirts. Meredith forced herself to walk away.

Chapter Five

"Can we go now? I'm starved."

Richard glanced up from the brief he was editing to see Laura standing in his office doorway. Her cream linen jacket was creased at the elbows and her skirt vaguely lined below her hips from sitting at her desk all afternoon. Her silk blouse, its collar casually unfurled, revealed an elegant collarbone. The desire to touch that skeletal necklace had prompted Richard's initial seduction of Laura two years ago. She had melted beneath his fingertips like snow. Now she smacked her briefcase urgently against her knees. Laura was never hungry. She wanted to go home.

"Sit down a moment. I just want to finish this paragraph." It would be cruel, Richard thought, to keep her waiting too long. Just another minute. Just to assert control. Laura perched on the edge of his gray couch and fidgeted with the briefcase handle.

"There. I'll do the rest after dinner. Since you're starving." He stood and stretched, his crisp shirt pulling up to tug tightly across his ribs and chest. Laura was watching him, and he could feel the physical twinge of their sexual connection, almost like pain. He lifted his charcoal pin-striped jacket from its hanger and slipped it on. Laura stood and straightened his collar. The perfect couple, he thought, feeling again the twist of her nearness.

"After you," he said, touching her elbow. "I thought the Atwood Café tonight. Then straight to the train. No loitering."

Smiling graciously, he held the elevator door and touched her back. Although Laura was consummately vicious in her professional life, after hours she liked someone to take care of her. He felt her arm begin to relax against his as the elevator plunged fifty floors to the lobby, a dramatically long fall strictly controlled by cables and pullies.

"Will you be all right in those heels?" he asked.

She smiled. "It's only a few blocks. I'll switch before I go to the train."

Strolling across Michigan Avenue, Richard enjoyed the heat and the bustle. The law firm was chilly and quiet, each lawyer sealed in his marble slot, secretaries silently stroking their computer keyboards. It was good to feel the real temperature of the air, and to hear real people talking to each other companionably. Again Richard held the door, and they entered the restaurant.

"Mr. Orwell, right this way. I have your table ready." The maitre d' escorted them to a booth in the back, a small fringed lamp barely illuminating the white tablecloth.

"Please bring some bread and a bottle of chardonnay. The lady is famished."

Next to him on the bench, Laura rested her head against his shoulder. He pushed his leg against hers. "I do adore you, Richard," she sighed.

The waiter approached with bread and wine. Laura sat up.

"Two grilled salmons please, and the house salads," Richard ordered for them both. "Now, eat some bread, Laura. It's not good to go all day without food. We'll get you home soon enough."

Laura crumbled a slice of bread and sipped her wine. "I'm sorry," she said. "Do you mind?"

"Of course I mind. I can't stand the idea of your living with another man. Every time I think of you together, I feel this horrible warmth, as if my veins have ruptured and the blood is filling my skin."

"Richard, that is disgusting." She smiled slightly. "You know Lewis and I are not together, not like that. You should see us, it's pathetic. I come home, and we ignore each other or spit a few words, and we spend the rest of the night in different parts of the house. It's awful living there. I believe we truly hate each other now, or at least I hate Lewis -- I'm not sure if he is capable of any powerful emotion. Can you imagine coming home every night to the person you most despise in the world, whom you once loved -- once -- but who now sends prickles down your spine, prickles of anger and revulsion? And that nauseating mother of his is there, over for dinner, taking care of my child, plotting with him every time I turn around. But I can't leave, I can't, not until the divorce is final. I can't leave without Marie. I have to show the judge just how much she means to me, how far

33

I'm willing to go to keep her with me. You know if I leave, they'll make this thing drag on and on, and before you know it she'll have been living away from me for six months, a year, maybe more. And that would give Lewis such an advantage."

"But, if you had your own apartment --   ." Richard paused. He would not beg, it was degrading. "Then you and I could spend more time together," he continued calmly. "Entire nights. Imagine."

"That would be heaven." Laura's eyes softened. "But we just have to be patient. Once I know I have done everything I can to keep Marie, once, God willing, I have Marie with me, then you and I can be together all the time. I'm sorry, Richard. I know you're impatient. Thank God you're impatient, thank God that you want us."

"Of course I want you." Richard held Laura's face, and he kissed her, a long, deep, ravishing kiss. She was bright and lovely and strong. He would never give her up. He just had to think of a way to pry her from that awkward child. Marie was the only obstacle between them. And Laura was right. He was indeed losing patience. After dinner, they parted in front of the restaurant. Laura turned west, for the train. Richard walked north toward the office, but then he changed his mind and continued home. He was too distracted to work. He had waited two years for Laura to arrive at this point, eager to divorce her husband and marry him. He was not much of a man if he now allowed a female infant to win the game.

Laura pressed the button on the automatic garage door opener. Although tired after her long day, she had walked straight from the train station to the garage and then dragged herself to the grocery store. Now she was finally home. The humming motor guided the old door up its tracks. Her headlights shone on Lewis's bicycle and an assortment of rakes and snow shovels and beach toys strewn along the side. She would have to speak to Angelica about straightening this mess. That woman had been working for them for so long, she was beginning to take advantage. Surely she couldn't be busy all day just cleaning the house and caring for one small child. And it wouldn't be too much for her to pick up a gallon of milk once in a while. She could walk to the store, it wasn't far, and they would pay her back. She needed to take some initiative. Laura shut off the car and the headlights, and the garage went black. It wasn't usually this black, was it? Stiff in the locked car, she imagined a man lurking in the darkness, leaping out to stick a knife to her throat. Fumbling for her purse and briefcase and the plastic gallon of milk, she admonished herself, she was in Winnetka, for heaven's sake, this was absurd. Opening her car door, the interior light cast a brief glow, and she glanced quickly about her. No one was waiting to attack her, of course, she was quite safe. The ceiling light bulb had burned out again, that was all. She had to do every little thing herself.

Laura walked through the dark to the kitchen door. By now Marie was probably in bed, and Laura had missed her chance. She put down the milk and fumbled with the back door key. She passed through the kitchen and the dining room, into the living room, where Lewis, his feet on the white couch, sat reading a book. He turned a page and glanced up.

"We'd given up on you. Mother's upstairs bathing Marie."

Laura clenched her fists. She had slaved all day, slogging through reams of paper, enduring hostile adversaries and neurotic clients, all to reach this moment, when the day was over, the work was almost done, and she could snatch a few human minutes with her child. It was one thing if Marie were asleep. It was quite another to allow her harpy mother-in-law to steal her one bit of joy. Laura dropped her things, rushed to the second floor, and flung open the bathroom door.

"Close that, she'll catch a chill!"

Laura entered the tiny bathroom and shut the door behind her. Her chest tightened. "Hello, Viola. You can leave now."

"Why, no thank you, Dear. We're having too much fun here, aren't you and Grandma having fun, Little Darling?" Viola filled a red plastic cup with water and poured it over Marie's raised knee. Marie stared, her blue eyes round.

"That's not the point. She's my daughter. And if I say get out, then you do it. I've been working hard all day. I want to spend some time with her now."

Viola stood. Her dyed red head came barely to Laura's shoulder. She shook a claw at her daughter-in-law. "You don't know what's good for this child, and you don't care. She's my granddaughter, and I'm entitled to spend some time with her. Lewis said I could. She's his child too."

All Laura would have to do was push. Viola wore little brown heeled leather shoes and a neatly pressed blue cotton dress. Her hair had been plastered in place at one of those beauty shops that caters to old ladies. The whole bathroom reeked of old lady, hairspray and rouge and cheap toilette water. If Laura gave her one good shove, she would topple into the bathtub and crack her head on the tile wall and slide into the water. Her dress would be wet and her hair would come unglued. But she would land on Marie, of course. With bare self-control, Laura opened the door, grabbed Viola's shoulders, twisted her around, shoved her out, and slammed the door shut. She heard the soft thud on the hallway carpeting and the thin sound of the old woman whining. Heavy feet mounted the stairs. Marie stood up in the shallow water and howled.

"It's all right, Sweetie, Mommy's here now. Are you having a nice bath? Here comes a boat, right up your leg!"

As Marie subsided, Laura could hear shuffling outside. "Your hip's not broken, Mother, I'm sure of that. Now, lean on me, that's right, up you go. I know, it's just terrible. We won't have to put up with this much longer."

It was a conspiracy, Lewis and Mother together again, against Lewis's wife, the encroaching woman, the outsider. They would probably report this to their lawyer, how the ogre had pushed poor Grandma down in front of the child, never mind that Grandma and Daddy had teamed up to keep Laura from doing more than pay for the beautiful house and the private babysitter and the pediatrician and every other damn thing they took for granted. But she wasn't good enough to raise Marie, only to pay for her, and all their luxuries.

Marie had her fist in her mouth, and she was shivering. Laura felt the water. It was cold. Some grandma she was. She wrapped a clean towel around Marie's shoulders and lifted her out.

"Come on, Sweetie. Come to Mama. Give Mommy a love."

Obediently, Marie rested her damp head on her mother's shoulder. Laura felt the child's generous warmth seep into her, and she clung to the baby, her own body responsively softening. "Let's go get into your nightie, and then bed. It's awfully late for little girls!"

Pink teddy bears danced on Marie's walls as Laura set her daughter on the rocking chair. "You stay there, and Mommy will find you a nice cozy nightie." Rummaging in the dresser, Laura found Marie's favorite, a short-sleeved cotton nightshirt stamped with a faded picture of Cinderella in her ball gown. She reached in the closet for a girl diaper, white plastic with pink rosebuds. Marie sat patiently, wrapped in her towel. "Now, slide down, and we'll get you all set."

Marie's stomach pooched over the diaper waist, and Laura slipped the nightgown over her head. Laura reached into the crib for the bunny blanket, settled into the rocking chair, and drew Marie to her. She began to rock, holding her daughter. Marie stuck her thumb in her mouth and began, slowly and methodically, to tickle her nose with the blanket. Laura rocked. This is what mattered. Only this.

They rocked for a long time. Laura heard Viola's raspy whisper in the hall. Block it out, she thought, it doesn't matter. Hold your baby tight. The warm breeze through the open windows felt like a gentle breath. Laura rocked, and her own eyes closed, and she felt Marie's head drooping heavily against her. Finally, she struggled to her feet, carrying the dead weight stiffly, so as not to disturb her, and laid Marie on the teddy bear sheet. Marie stretched. Tenderly, Laura stroked her back.

"Sweet dreams, Angel. See you in the morning."

Laura picked up the damp towel and left the room. Outside in the dark hallway, Lewis lurked, waiting for her.

"I put Mother in the guest room. She wanted to go home, but I didn't think she should drive. She was too shaken up."

"Fine." Laura tossed the towel to Lewis, walked to her own bedroom, and shut the door. She turned on the fan and began to strip off her clothes, the jacket and the silk blouse and the linen skirt and the sticky stockings. She just hoped Viola would sleep late, so she wouldn't have to watch her gumming her cornflakes. She didn't think she could bear it.

Chapter Six

Laura dreamed she had opened the door of the closet in her office. The closet was deep, dense with high heels and heaps of papers and suspended sweaters, wooly gray arms brushing her face like spiders. When she reached up to take a sweater, a man emerged from within the closet, his hands large and threatening and groping for her. She tried to back up, but she could not move, she was mired in the papers or she was paralyzed, and the man's hands were closing on her waist. She screamed, and the sound of her own voice and the desperate need to escape the man awakened her.

She knew instantly that it had been a dream, and she was hardly afraid, but annoyed with herself for breaking her sleep. Through the whir of the window fan she thought she heard Marie whimpering, restless in her own damp sleep, perhaps dreaming her own childish nightmare. What would a baby's nightmare be? Did monsters exist in Marie's mind, were they men or crocodiles or dogs or old women? Laura could go in to her, she could comfort Marie as no one ever comforted Laura. Mommy is here. There, there, go to sleep, Mommy won't let anything bad happen to you, you are safe in your own bed. But children must develop their own resources, they must learn self-reliance. She pulled the sheet up around her shoulders and turned over.

40

Laura's eyes shot open. Damn, she had forgotten to review the contracts for the deposition tomorrow. She sat up and checked the clock. Three-ten. She heard footsteps in the hall, Grandma Witch on the prowl for a midnight snack, no doubt. Laura had left her briefcase at the foot of the stairs. Well, she wasn't about to face Viola, not on half a night's sleep. She might bluff her way through the deposition, but she could not possibly deal with Viola at three a.m. Again, Laura stretched out on her bed and closed her eyes. Eventually, she slept.

At seven, Laura's radio alarm went off, Bach it was, precise and relentless. Keep me moving, Johann, she thought, and she stumbled into the bathroom. Shower, teeth, dress, hair, make-up, earrings, shoes, coffee, bye-bye, every morning for years. When she stepped, moist and cool, from the bathroom, Lewis was standing outside the door. She gripped her robe tightly around herself. He always seemed to be waiting for her.

"Do you have Marie?" he asked.

"Of course not. I was in the shower. Isn't she in bed?"

"No."

"Well, I obviously don't have her. Ask your mother. She's probably feeding her some perfect 1955 baby breakfast." Laura turned toward her bedroom.

"My mother's not here. She left a note in the kitchen, she said she didn't want to see you, so she left early."

"That's a relief." Laura ruffled her wet hair. "Look, Lewis, I've got to get ready for work. Can't you handle this? Marie must have climbed out of her crib, and she's playing someplace in the house. I know she doesn't usually do it, but she's old enough, and there's a first time for everything. Call her, look around, you're an intelligent man." Laura walked into her bedroom and shut the door. She had to stay on schedule to make the express train.

When she emerged, suited and perfect, Lewis was there again. "I can't find her. Do you think she could have opened the front door?"

Laura hesitated. "No. But if your mother was careless maybe Marie got out of bed and found the door hanging open."

Laura hurried downstairs and checked the doors. They were both tightly closed, and the back door was latched from the inside. Lewis must have checked it before he went to bed. The front door locked automatically, but it could also be bolted either from the inside with a knob, or from the outside with the front door key. It was not bolted.

"Did you close the front door? Because I'm sure Marie couldn't have shut it behind her."

"No. The doors were closed when I came down."

The telephone rang. Laura released an exasperated sigh. "That must be your mother saying, 'Oh, by the way, when I left, I took your daughter with me.' You get it."

Lewis answered the phone in the hall, and Laura went into the kitchen to make coffee. A few minutes later, he joined her. His face was white.

"That was Angelica. She's still sick, she can't come in today. And I called Mom. She doesn't have Marie."

"What do you mean she doesn't have her? She must have her. I knew that woman wanted to take my baby away from me, but I didn't think she was capable of kidnapping. What do you know about this? Is this some scheme you two have cooked up? Because it's not clever, Lewis, it's not going to work. Look, I have work to do today, I don't have time for this."

Lewis grabbed Laura's shoulders. "I'm telling you, my mother didn't take her. She wouldn't do something like that. She wanted to come right over, but I wouldn't let her. She was as worried as I am."

"That I'd believe. Look, I'm checking the house myself. And if she's not here and you persist in this dumb act, I'm calling the police. Little girls do not simply vanish into thin air in the middle of the night."

Laura hurried up the stairs. In her vast experience as a partner at Winters & Early, she had handled nervous clients, nasty attorneys, depositions and trials and trips to foreign countries. She had handled them all reasonably and responsibly, and with a minimum of fuss. But now she was frightened. Something was going on here. Either Lewis was conning her, or her mother-in-law was punishing her, or something much worse had happened. Maybe, somehow, Marie really was missing.

At the top of the stairs, Laura leaned over the banister. "Lewis, go outside and check the yard and walk around the block. Maybe somehow she wandered away."

"Okay." Laura went into Marie's bedroom. The teddy bears on the walls and curtains frolicked around her. Gripping the rail, she stared into the vacant crib. The bears on the sheet lay flat and silent. A fuzzy stuffed duck rested listlessly in one corner, and an afghan lay crumpled at the foot. Perhaps her daughter was under it. Perhaps somehow she had become so tiny she would fit, tightly curled, beneath the small heap. Laura lifted the afghan. But Marie and her bunny blanket were gone.

Marie must have climbed out of bed with her blanket, curled up in a closet or under a chair, and gone back to sleep. Lewis had simply overlooked her. That must be it, that had to be it. In a few days she would laugh over this, even by this afternoon the whole incident would have become simply another story to tell Richard about Lewis's aggravating incompetence. Laura flung open the closet door to reveal an array of lavender and rose and yellow summer dresses, flowers and lace, gardens and sunshine. On the floor stood a package of disposable diapers and three neatly aligned pairs of shoes, Marie's pink sandals and her sneakers and her sparkly party shoes. But Marie was not there.

Laura jerked open Marie's dresser drawers. Her ruffled shorts and rainbow tee shirts, her lace-trimmed socks and her pink tutu bathing suit, everything was clean and neatly folded and in place. If Lewis or Viola had taken Marie, surely they would have taken her clothes. Or perhaps they were too clever for that. They could always buy new things. The only irreplaceable object was the bunny blanket, and that was missing too.

Laura stood uncertainly in the middle of the room. Something kept her from leaving, from beginning a methodical search of the rest of the house. Her eyes combed the room, the porcelain dolls, the alphabet blocks, the white rocking chair, the frilled lamp, and the open windows, admitting a warm, clean breeze. The open windows. Hesitantly, Laura approached the window opposite Marie's crib, the window facing the side of the house. The glass was raised to its full height, revealing the complete expanse of flimsy screen, all that had separated Marie from the rest of the entire world. As Laura stared at the screen, her breath stopped.

The screen was broken. Its edges rested against the metal frame, but they were no longer attached to it. Frantic, Laura pushed against the mesh to look out the window. The bottom and sides of the screen came completely away, creating a clear view of the ground. But Marie was not lying broken and bleeding on the flagstone path. She had not fallen from the window. Laura leaned back. The screen edges again rested neatly against the frame. There were no uneven tears, no awkward bulges. The edges were perfectly square, as if they had been cleanly severed with a sharp knife. Laura stood at the window. Her eyes grew round, and she screamed and screamed and screamed.

Chapter Seven

The telephone rang. "Meredith Bennett."

"Hi, Meredith. It's Joe Field."

"Hello, Detective. What's up?" Meredith set her coffee cup back down on her desk and scooted forward. Although Joe worked in Winnetka, generally a quiet suburb, detectives usually called the state's Attorneys office regarding tricky points of law or serious crimes.

"Well, we have a missing baby girl up here, eighteen months old, at 908 Cherry. It looks ugly, her bedroom screen's been cut, and the parents are pretty shook up. I'm organizing a search of the vicinity, and I was wondering if you could come down to the scene and help us out with some of the more important witness interviews. It sure would be a big help, especially with talking to the parents and everything -- I want to make sure it gets handled right."

"I'm glad you called, Joe. I'll try to get somebody to cover for me, and I'll be right there."

"Great. It's 908 Cherry, the name's Sumner, baby Marie, parents Laura and Lewis."

"Okay. See you in fifteen minutes."

Meredith's heart was racing. She was drowning in misdemeanors, and this was the rope that would rescue her, at least haul her out for a minute so that she could take a gulp of air. She would try to be home on time for

Maggie and Lucy, but they were getting older, and she needed this, she needed a new experience.

And an eighteen-month-old girl -- the poor parents must be terrified. She pictured Lucy at that age, still a baby, but walking, beginning to talk, understanding. The little girl and her mother would have bonded so tightly, they would practically be one person. The mother would feel her child's vulnerability keenly and desperately need to protect her. She must be going berserk, and Meredith could talk to her mother-to-mother, comfort her, calm her down. She would press the father harder. Meredith wasn't about to leap to conclusions, but she read the newspaper. North Shore or South Side, nine times out of ten, the man of the house had caused the bloody mess on the living room floor.

Meredith grabbed her purse and her briefcase and peeked around her friend Amy Grossman's doorway. "Believe it or not, we've got a possible kidnapping in Winnetka, and they need some help with witness interviews. Could you possibly handle Courtroom F for me this morning?"

"Sure, I've done F before. Six months probation and a fifty dollar fine, right? Don't blow a gasket with all this excitement, and I expect a full report when you get back."

"Thanks, you're an angel. The files are on my desk."

She rushed down the rubber stairs, past the popcorn stand and the metal detectors, and out to the parking garage.

Driving north on Sheridan Road, Meredith admired the enormous oaks heavy with leaves, an emerald awning in the sharp summer sun. She knew that the mansions she passed here along the lake were fantastically expensive. Once, when she was still married to Dr. Alexander, she might have imagined herself, wine spritzer hoisted in a toast to the good life, lounging on her own private beach after an exhausting day of eating oriental chicken salad and having her toenails painted. Now, the property taxes on a detached garage exceeded her annual salary. Even Alexander and the new improved Mrs. Bennett, in their Kenilworth tudor complete with master bedroom suite, convection oven, and professionally manicured half-acre, could not manage riparian. She turned west on Cherry. Apparently, neither could the Sumners, she thought, as the houses became more modest four-bedroom types, though Meredith was certain that at this moment they would trade the most exquisite beachfront villa for their daughter's familiar smile. Laura and Lewis Sumner. The names sounded familiar, but she simply could not place them. Maybe she'd met them once at a cocktail party, back in the old days.

Even without the legions of police cars and evidence vans, 908 Cherry stood out from its neighbors. The house looked as if the earth were slowly consuming it. Ivy vines glued their tentacles to the stucco and clawed at the second floor windows. The wood trim had peeled in flaky green splotches, and the grass in the front yard folded under its own weight. A small dirt bed next to the front path displayed only dandelions and gangly, vaguely adorned protrusions. Even Meredith had bought a flat of petunias at the grocery store and stuck them around her front bushes. No one had bothered with that here.

She emerged from her car, approached several paces along the flagstone walk, and then stopped still. Suddenly, she did not want to go into the house. Since receiving the phone call from Joe Field, she had convinced herself that, although the parents were worried, really, everything was fine. After all, this was Winnetka -- and children disappear every day, only to turn up safe a few hours later. They wander off and get lost or go exploring or fall asleep in a secret nook. But rarely does anything serious befall them. She had felt sure she could reassure the parents and ask a few probing questions, and then the child would reappear intact, via Joe and his squadron or of its own accord, if not in time for the afternoon court call, certainly before dinner.

But now that she saw the house, Meredith was not so certain. Something was wrong here. And if that baby were truly missing or maimed or dead, if some maniac had taken it, the suffering she would encounter here would be terrible beyond imagination. Robotlike, her feet resumed the path. She was here to do a job, and she must do it, she must help them if she could. Her finger reached for the doorbell, and she pushed it.

Detective Joe Field opened the screen door. Meredith stepped through the cozy hallway and past the carpeted stairway into the living room, bare oak floors and a stiff white couch, as if two completely different and uncompromising consciousnesses had furnished the two areas.

A woman sat on the couch. Laura Sumner. She was tall and willowy, impeccably dressed in a beige summer suit, a slender gold chain circling her throat. But her skin was gray-white, her eyes staring, and she clutched a tiny pair of pink sneakers studded with plastic hearts. She looked elegant, professional, and completely undone.

"Mrs. Sumner, this is Meredith Bennett. Meredith, Laura Sumner," said Joe. "Ms. Bennett is a state's attorney. She's here to talk to you while we search the vicinity."

"Hello, Mrs. Sumner. We'll do everything we can to find your daughter. I know how anxious you must be." Meredith leaned forward to squeeze her shoulder comfortingly.

The woman flinched. "Don't patronize me. You know nothing about my anxiety. You couldn't possibly," she said. Meredith reddened and backed up a step. Then she remembered. It hit her like Laura's unprovoked slap. The newspaper. This was the great Laura Sumner, Superwoman, unattainable icon for every working woman in the Chicago metropolitan area. And brought to ground at last.

"This is Lewis Sumner." Joe indicated a man with receding gray-brown hair, thick glasses, and a small paunch imperfectly hidden under a worn sport shirt and blue jeans. All Laura's glamour had apparently failed her in the male department. He sat folded into a peach wing chair in the corner of the room, like a disappointing child trying to conceal the misdemeanor of his existence. This was Mr. Superwoman, the Northwestern professor. Despite her earlier suspicions of boyfriends and husbands in domestic violence situations, he had Meredith's immediate sympathy. She judged him the more forthright and less hostile of the pair, the more likely to provide helpful information.

"Is there a quiet room where we could talk?" she asked him.

Lewis led her into a dark, book-lined, deeply comforting den. He eased behind a large oak desk cluttered with books and papers, and he motioned her to a leather arm chair.

"You do a lot of reading."

"Yes. I'm an assistant professor of sociology at Northwestern, and I do a lot of work at home."

"And your wife?" Meredith remembered from the newspaper article, but she wanted to double check.

"Laura is a partner at Winters & Early. Look, I'm sorry, but could we get down to it? I'm going out of my mind. Some lunatic may have my daughter, and I don't want to waste time."

"Do you have a picture of her that we could borrow?" Lewis turned to the bookshelf and picked up a snapshot in a plain plexiglass frame. "This is Marie. She walks, of course, as you see, but she doesn't talk much yet. I'm sure she'll catch up later."

"She's a lovely child. She looks like you," Meredith said kindly, glancing between the frozen cherub and her worn, graying father.

Lewis stared at the photograph. "Do you really think so?" he asked. "Frankly, I've never been able to see it."

He looked as if the smallest touch would deflate him. Meredith wished she could reach across his desk and hug him for a moment, one human to another. He obviously wasn't going to get much comfort from his wife.

"Tell me what happened this morning," she said instead, gently, trying to proceed as he wished.

Presumably, he had already recited this information to the police, and he was ready. "I got up as usual, around seven. Since Marie was quiet, I got dressed, and then I went to check her. She wasn't there. She can climb out of the crib, but she doesn't usually do it. Laura and I searched the house, and we couldn't find her anywhere, and all the doors were closed and locked. I decided to look around the neighborhood, just in case she'd managed somehow to get out the front door and shut it behind her. You see, the front door wasn't bolted, though it locks automatically when you close it. The kitchen door was latched from the inside. She couldn't have left that way."

"Why wasn't the front door bolted?"

My mother stayed here overnight last night. She left early, before we got up. I know, I thought of that of course, I've called her. She doesn't have Marie. Anyway, Laura went back upstairs to search again. That's when she noticed the screen on Marie's window. It was cut. It seems impossible, but someone must have come in during the night and taken her."

52

"Did you hear anything last night?"

"No. I've wracked my brain, but the fan was on, making its usual racket, and I'm a sound sleeper." He hesitated. "My bedroom isn't next to Marie's either -- Laura's is." He paused. " We're getting divorced. We still live together because we both want full custody of Marie."

The superwoman, beacon-to-all-women article had failed to mention that small fact. And that changed everything. "I don't want to jump to conclusions," Meredith said carefully, "but do you think it's possible that your wife might have something to do with this? I'm sure you're aware that people do desperate things to keep their children."

Lewis shook his head. "I just don't know. She seems genuinely upset. But I just don't know."

"You didn't hear her leave last night?"

"No, but my mother left, and I didn't hear her. My mother came over yesterday evening to visit. When Laura came home, they had a fight. Laura actually pushed the old lady down, if you can believe it, and she was too upset to drive home. She slept in the guest room, or, apparently couldn't sleep, and that's why she left early." He hesitated. "We had a painter here yesterday, Mike Ramsey. He's just a neighborhood kid, he seems like a nice guy, but quiet. He was working outside Marie's room yesterday. He left his ladder in the backyard, lying down behind the swing."

"Was it still in the same place this morning?"

"I think so, it wasn't propped against the house or anything, but I can't be sure it was in exactly the same place. You'll have to ask him."

"Is he here now?"

"No. That's a little weird, since he was supposed to work today, but you know how handymen are, you're never sure when they'll show up. Or maybe he saw all the police and got scared."

"That's all right. Just jot down his name and address for me. I'll need your mother's too. And you must have a babysitter. Or are you off work for the summer?"

"No, we do have a sitter. Her name is Angelica Vasquez. She called in sick today."

"Is that unusual?"

"Not really. She's a responsible person, but she does get sick occasionally, or maybe she just needs a day off, I don't know. Since my hours are fairly flexible, I can usually cover for it." He hesitated. "I believe she was having her period. Maybe it was a rough one."

"All right, I'll need her address and phone number too. Mr. Sumner, excuse the question, but I need to ask. Does your wife have a -- boyfriend?"

Lewis smiled wanly. "No good word for that social position, is there?" He paused. "I don't really know. I think you should discuss that with her."

"Okay. What about you? Do you have a girlfriend?"

"No. No girlfriend."

She actually felt relieved. What was she thinking? She stood up.

"Thank you, Mr. Sumner. One more thing. Did you leave the house at any time last night?"

"No, of course not. I am not involved in Marie's disappearance in any way."

"Okay. I just had to check. Please get me those names, addresses, and phone numbers, and send in your wife."

Meredith watched Lewis's crumpled figure emerge from behind his desk. She gritted her teeth and waited for Laura.

At a skewed angle, Richard glimpsed, in his office window, the shade of his own reflection. Tall and muscular in his navy striped suit, his golden head now half silver, Richard looked, he knew, much as his lawyer father had looked before him. They were both Yale graduates, both partners at top law firms, men of power and prestige. But unlike his father, who had two, Richard had never possessed a wife. He had been too busy with work for foolish romance. Falling in love with Laura was an unexpected perk, the result of long, late hours together spent tangling with the same problems and pressures. In her, Richard had found a female version of himself. The existence of her husband, and later, a child, had created more of an impediment than Richard had anticipated. He wanted to marry Laura, Laura alone. Together, they made an impressive team.

Between the two windows on the wall opposite his desk Richard had hung an abstract oil painting, black dribbles and a dramatic red slash, which he had purchased in a prominent River North gallery one rainy afternoon eight years ago. He had needed a painting for his new corner office, and he refused to be cowed by the gallery's alien atmosphere. He knew that despite its pretensions of aesthetic chic and obscure, deep meaning, a gallery was a business, in existence to please those with money to spend. He stated the dimensions of the painting he required and that he wanted no nudes or violence, nothing that would evoke a strong emotional response. The dealer buzzed Richard into the back room, lined with rows of plastic-sheathed canvases, and quickly produced several paintings of the right size and degree of abstraction. Richard asked his decorator to make the final selection for him, and then he purchased it. In spite of his lack of interest in art, he found that he did respond to the painting, that staring at it as he talked on the phone made him more forceful. Eyeing the garish red stain, Richard picked up his telephone and dialed Laura's home number.

"Sumner residence," responded a gruff male voice, certainly not Lewis's. Lewis always sounded as if he had picked up the receiver accidentally and was afraid it might be hot.

"Laura Sumner, please. This is Richard Orwell, one of her partners."

"Just a minute. I'll see if she can come to the phone."

Richard heard shuffling and murmuring.
"Hello?"

"Laura, what's going on? It's ten o'clock, and they're waiting for you to start the deposition."

"Oh, God, Richard, I'm sorry. I completely forgot."

"What do you mean you forgot? This isn't like you."

"Oh, Richard." Laura began to weep, deep, aching sobs.

"My God, Laura. Whatever is the matter?"

"Someone has taken Marie." Gasping, she dropped the phone.

"Mr. Orwell?" The man had returned to the line. "This is Detective Field of the Winnetka Police Department. You're a partner of Mrs. Sumner's?"

"That's right." Richard paused. "I was concerned when she didn't show up for a deposition this morning. I never expected anything like this."

"All right, Sir. I'm afraid I'll have to ask you to leave this line free now. Goodbye."

"Goodbye."

Richard hung up and drew a long breath. Laura had sounded terribly upset. He had known, of course, that she was attached to the child, but she had also recognized that Marie was a burden, a distraction from her career and an impediment to her relationship with him. He would not have anticipated abject hysteria over its absence. But, one must, of course, feel concern for a missing child, or one would surely be a beast. He lifted his head and gazed at the painting, the black and the red. Children disappear all the time, usually taken by a parent in a divorce context, just the sort of situation Laura was in now. Richard could quite convincingly reassure Laura that Lewis had stashed Marie somewhere, that she was safe and happy and untraceable. Eventually, Lewis would disappear too, off to join Marie, and that would be that.

Of course, Laura need not continue to live with Lewis now that Marie was gone. Richard must give her a little time to think straight, but surely by the end of the week her anger at Lewis and her sense of the futility of locating a nondescript, nonverbal child would drive her into Richard's open arms. Once they were married, they would be so busy reigning over the law firm and taking fascinating vacations that she would soon forget the child altogether.

Richard walked down the hall to the conference room. The court reporter sat poised before her machine, the witness sipped coffee nervously, and opposing counsel leaped to his feet.

"This is ridiculous. I'm afraid we can't wait any longer. And it'll be a cold day in hell before you get us here again."

"I'm terribly sorry, David," Richard said smoothly. "I just called Ms. Sumner's home. Suffice it to say, only a family ·emergency could have kept her from her obligations to this case. She apologizes for the inconvenience to you, and she has asked me to fill in for her today. I think the best thing we can do for her and for our clients is to proceed. If you'll kindly give me just a moment to look over the file, we can begin."

Chapter Eight

Carolyn Ramsey stepped out on her front steps and peered down the street. She saw six parked police cars, and two men were talking in the Sumners' front yard. Mr. Brier from next door was strolling past the Sumners' too, pretending to walk the dog. He would stop and hail the men and say that he wanted to help. But all he really wanted was gossip, a good story out of someone else's misery.

"What's happening now, Mom?" Mike cracked the screen door.

"I don't know. Nothing good, that's for sure, with all those police. You get back. I do not want you going over there to work today, and that's final."

Mike backed into the house's protective darkness. Carolyn followed him into the kitchen, where he flopped onto a chair, his blue-jeaned knees akimbo, his chin plunged into his hands.

Mike was not the son Carolyn had expected. She was a good Christian woman from a decent family. She wore skirts and stockings and had her hair trimmed every six weeks. And she had always been a good mother to Mike, all through his growing up. She had driven him to school every day and picked him up to come straight home afterwards. She had bought him Halloween costumes and birthday cakes and Christmas presents, she had sent him to Sunday School, and she was his room mother every single year. When other women were letting their teenagers run wild, riding in each other's cars and staying out until all hours of the night, she had always kept Mike safe at home and made sure that he got a good night's sleep.

Cliff had not been much of a father, and he was undoubtedly the source of all of Mike's problems. He was a doctor, and it was hard to insist that he stay in for a quiet family evening when somebody's life was at stake. But she and Mike had been lonely. When Cliff started staying out late all the time, Carolyn had quit waiting around for him and shut him out of the bedroom too. She had seen his floozy nurse. A wife couldn't be expected to forgive that. When Cliff got sick, she was sorry, but she figured that might be justice. He wanted her company then, of course. Once he was stuck in the house and the nurse wouldn't have him, Carolyn was good enough again, good enough to wash him and change his sheets and feed him with a spoon, by the end. She hated to say it, but it was just as well when he died. She had loved him once, though. She still missed him sometimes.

Carolyn picked up a bottle of cleaning solution and a damp washcloth. She sprayed the counter and carefully rubbed the formica. At least she had Mike here, living with her again. That was a real comfort. They ate dinner together every night, and breakfast most mornings. Those perfect North Shore mothers with their ideal children couldn't say that. Their sons were up and out, they went away to Dartmouth or Princeton, and they only came home if they ran out of money. What Carolyn had accomplished was in many ways much better. She would have been so lonely living by herself. The only thing that had got her through the year Mike was away, lying to the neighbors, all those silent evenings, was knowing that it was temporary. She had to stay strong so that she could help him when he came home again.

Carolyn turned around. "I'm going to put on the teapot. It'll do us both some good."

That was it, she had to stay strong. Whatever had happened down at the Sumners', it had nothing to do with Mike. He had been over there yesterday, of course, but he was home for dinner. They had watched T.V. together, and then they went to bed.

She was a very light sleeper. When Mike was a baby, he just had to whimper, and she was out of bed like a shot. In the morning, Cliff would show up dressed in the kitchen, and there she would be with Mike in her arms, and Cliff would say, "When did you two get up?" He never heard a thing. But Carolyn always heard Mike. He couldn't possibly have left the house last night without her knowing.

The kettle boiled, a shrill scream. Carolyn turned off the stove and poured the steaming water over the teabag in Mike's mug. She dunked the bag a few times and then moved it to her own china cup. She stirred sugar into the mug, added a few tablespoons of milk, to cool it off, and set it in front of him. His face was gray and tired. He went to bed early last night, right after the nine o'clock news. Why did he look so tired?

"I didn't do it, Mom." Mike stared at her bleakly. "Mom, whatever it is, I didn't do it. You think I did, but I didn't."

Carolyn turned away. She sprayed the stove and started to scrub. "I don't know what you're talking about, Son."

"I was at the Sumners' yesterday, and now something's wrong, and you think I did it. But I didn't. I was here all night. You know that, right, Mom?"

"Of course I know that. Anyway, we don't even know what's happening down there. Some domestic squabble, no doubt. Lewis probably shoved her, and she hurt herself."

"Maybe Mrs. Sumner did something to him. Poisoned him, or something." Mike stared at her. "That's possible, you know."

"Don't be ridiculous." Carolyn squirted cleaner on the oven door.

The front doorbell rang.

Mike's mother stooped to return the bottle of cleaner to the wire basket attached to the inside of the cupboard door. She kept all her cleaning supplies there, where she could get to them easily. She folded the washcloth neatly and draped it over the faucet. She had always been like this, as long as Mike could remember. She made a plan, and she followed it to completion. She turned to face Mike. The doorbell rang again.

"We could just pretend we're not here, Mom," he said. "They don't know." But Mike could feel his heart beating, and he was sure that whoever was at the door could sense it too, the pulse of his body, hiding back here in the kitchen.

"Nonsense," said his mother, straightening her blouse. "I simply will not be rushed. A stranger appears uninvited on my doorstep, disturbing my work -- he can wait for a moment, that's all. It's only common courtesy."

Mike sat at the kitchen table as his mother's footsteps receded. She would open the front door, the police would come in, and they would arrest him. They would send him to prison, a real prison this time. But he couldn't go to prison, he couldn't face it, the fear, the isolation, and the pain.

He would leave, he thought. There was no law that said he had to sit here waiting to be arrested. He would just step out for a few minutes. He heard voices in the hall, his mother sounding remote and bizarrely cheery, and another woman. It was only another woman. Just relax, Mike, he thought, it'll be all right.

"Well, he wasn't feeling too well today, so I kept him home. All that hard work in the heat, you know, it's just too much. You sit here in the living room, and I'll see if he's well enough to talk to you."

Now was his chance. All he had to do was get up, turn the doorknob, and run. His mother would cover for him. She would just say he was throwing up or asleep in bed. But, what about his tapes? If they searched the house, they would find his tapes. He couldn't leave the house without them, and he couldn't get them from upstairs without passing the woman.

His mother came into the kitchen. "Mom . . ." His voice was shrill and unnatural, the plaintive call of a baby bird in the jaws of a cat.

"Just go talk to her a minute, Mike. She just wants to know if you saw anything yesterday, and why you didn't come in today. You were sick, just tell her you were sick. I don't think she knows anything. It'll be all right."

Lightly, Mike's mother touched his shoulder. That scared him more than anything. She never touched him, never, not since he was ten years old and he had yelled at her for holding his hand when they crossed the street. He didn't think she had ever touched his father.

Maybe she was up to something. Maybe she didn't like having men in the house. His father had been a strong man, bursting with intelligence and energy. Then he became a cripple, and then he died. Mike had never understood what had happened to him, and his mother wouldn't talk about it. But every week, she had made his father soup, and she had insisted that he eat it, the same way she had forced Mike to eat his soup. The way she still did. Mike looked at her. Her face had that tight, tense set, a plaster mask of stress that would crack and shatter when they were alone. He stood and moved to the back door.

"Mike?" A strange woman stood in the kitchen doorway. Uninvited, she had crossed the living room and walked down the narrow hallway to the back of the house, the private part. "I'm Ms. Bennett. Won't you sit down?"

Mike sat. The woman was middle-aged, with brown hair and glasses and a brown suit. She looked old and hot and dumpy. He could hear his mother silently fume as Ms. Bennett took over her house.

"What's this about, anyway?" his mother blurted. "Some trouble at the Sumners', I gather?"

"I'm afraid so. It seems that the little girl, Marie, is missing." Mike felt his stomach drop, and his mother leaned against the counter behind her to support herself. "Did you see or hear anything unusual last night or early this morning, Mrs. Ramsey?"

"No. Nothing at all." Her face was bloodless.

"Were you home all of last night?"

"Yes, of course. Where would I be? My son and I were both here, together."

"Thank you, Mrs. Ramsey. I would like to talk to your son alone now, if I might."

Mike told Ms. Bennett his story. He had worked all day, and everything seemed fine. Yes, he had scraped around Marie's window. The window was open, but the screen was down, and it looked tight, but he hadn't tried it. He didn't need to open anything, he was just doing outside work, strictly outside. He had left the ladder by the hedge, and he had gone home around five o'clock. No, he had not gone back to the Sumners', why would he? He was sick this morning, and he had forgotten to call. That's all. He sat on his hands, to keep them still.

Ms. Bennett reached into her briefcase. She pulled out a plastic bag and dangled it before his face.

"Is this yours?"

He bit his lip. "Could be."

"Did you use a knife like this yesterday when you were scraping paint around Marie's window?" It was a short knife with a thick wooden handle and a strong, sharp blade.

"Yeah, I think so. What about it?"

"Just that we found this knife on Marie's window sill this morning. It was behind the curtains. On the inside."

Mike felt his heart thumping in his chest, his palms slick against the chair seat. "I didn't put it there. I told you, I never went into that little girl's room. I guess I just forgot that knife up there on the window ledge, and somebody else brought it inside. Lots of workmen leave their tools around. It's not a crime."

"But you took the ladder down."

"Yeah. Mr. Sumner told me to." He hesitated. "Did somebody move it?"

"A good question, Mike. Frankly, we can't tell. I would like you to come back to the Sumners' with me and take a look at the ladder, see if it's where you left it."

"I told you, I left it against the hedge."

"I know, but I want you to take a look. It might be at a different angle, or shifted in position somehow. Your observations could help us find Marie. All right?"

Ms. Bennett stood up.   Reluctantly, Mike followed her down the hall, past his mother, who was dusting the living room.   "Mike will be back in a minute," said Ms. Bennett.   "He's going to help us over at the Sumners'."

Hanging his head, he followed Ms. Bennett down the sidewalk. They passed Mr. Brier and his smutty little weasel dog, and Mrs. Pane, watering her lawn with a hose instead of just turning on the sprinkler, and a knot of housewives gathered near the Sumners' house as their toddlers scooted up and down on plastic horses and brightly colored cars.   "You just have to watch your children every minute, in this day and age," one of the women said.

"So many weirdos around," said another. "I don't know what this world is coming to."   He felt their eyes pinned to his skin as he passed.   Please, don't let them find out about me, he prayed.

When he got to the Sumners', Ms. Bennett led him down the path to the backyard. He glanced at the ladder. "It's just where I left it," he said.

"Are you sure, Mike? Take a careful look."

He walked slowly around the ladder, trying to appear as if he were studying every millimeter of its position.

"Yup," he said. "It's just where I left it."

"Thank you, Mike. You've been very helpful. We'll need to get a formal statement from you later, but for now, you can go home. Talk to you soon."

Mike turned and walked back home to face his mother.

Chapter Nine

Meredith drove south on Ridge toward Chicago. Joe Field had two officers ringing doorbells along Cherry, trying to find out if anyone had heard or seen anything last night that might be linked to Marie's disappearance. The other police and Lewis Sumner were literally beating the bushes, searching for Marie. Perhaps Laura Sumner had the hardest job, waiting in the house for phone calls. Her conversation with Meredith had been predictably laced with hostility and despair, as she repeatedly insinuated that Meredith and her colleagues were intellectually incapable of locating a neon sign, let alone a missing baby girl. Laura had indignantly denied having a lover, and had otherwise corroborated Lewis's story in every respect. She also stated that she had not left the house last night, and that she had nothing to do with Marie's disappearance. Meredith had left her huddled in a miserable ball on the living room couch.

Meredith considered her new acquaintances. The painter Mike Ramsey and his mother Carolyn struck her as an odd, nervy pair. The police were running a background check on Mike and on Angelica Vasquez, the babysitter. Lewis Sumner seemed suitably attached to his child and genuinely shaken by her disappearance. Although hardly the teen idol type, Meredith had to admit that his middle-aged professorial attractions managed to tug both her maternal and sexual instincts. Certainly he deserved an upgrade from Laura, who was stiff and nasty, used to playing tough and getting her own way. Her apparent despair could simply constitute Act I in an elaborate plan to avoid the custody dispute and keep Marie for herself. Lewis seemed to consider that a possibility. But Meredith had trouble imagining a woman as career-driven as Laura risking the legal and professional ramifications of committing a crime to keep her baby.

Meredith stopped in front of number twelve forty-one, a standard brick and cement Rogers Park apartment building, squatty and stubbornly permanent. Crabgrass erupted from the dry yard, and neglected yews sprawled over the front windows. They must use the same gardener as Lewis and Laura, Meredith thought, grinning. She locked her car, walked up the cement path, and rang the first doorbell, labeled "V. Sumner."

"Who's there?" a disembodied voice quavered.

"Mrs. Sumner?" Meredith shouted awkwardly into the wooden door. "I'm Meredith Bennett, a state's attorney. I'm here about your granddaughter. May I talk with you a moment?"

A bolt turned, and the door opened. Heavily sprayed red hair capped Viola Sumner's pouchy face and stooped body like parrot feathers on a vulture. Her bosom, enrobed in an ivory blouse, sagged over her waist. "Please come in," she nodded apologetically. "I'm sorry. I've never gotten used to those intercom things."

Meredith entered the tiny living room. An old brown couch leaned against the wall, opposite a portable T.V. on a metal stand and a maple magazine table stuffed with Reader's Digests. Despite the July heat, the windows were closed.

"Would you like some iced tea?"

"Yes, please." Meredith followed Viola down a dim passage into a yellowing kitchen.

"I'm just petrified about Marie. Of course, I can't help wondering -- have you met my daughter-in-law? Well, of course you have, and I'm sure you must know about the divorce and the fight over Marie. I hate to speak ill of anyone, and Laura may be suffering now, but -- well, look at my arm." Viola turned up her sleeve to reveal a light bruise, navy-green under baggy skin. "Laura did that to me last night. She pushed me, an old lady, trying to give my only grandchild a bath because her mother was too busy being a big shot to come home at a reasonable hour and care for her family." Mrs. Sumner sank down in a kitchen chair and shoved a dish of sourballs toward Meredith.

"But Laura wants custody of Marie?"

"That's what she says, but I tell you, she doesn't give that poor baby the time of day. The only mother Marie has ever known is that little Mexican babysitter, and I call that a shame. Laura just likes to own things. She made this child, it belongs to her, and she's going to keep it, and to hell with anyone else, if you'll excuse the expression. That woman's been nothing but trouble since the day Lewis met her, and the divorce won't even get rid of her. They'll always be tied together through that child, she'll always have her skinny fingers in the pot, stirring it up and ruining everybody's lives."

"Do you think it's possible that Laura might have taken Marie herself and hidden her away somewhere?"

"I don't know. She could have done it. She could have rented an apartment and hired a babysitter. She's got plenty of money, and she certainly wouldn't care what that did to Lewis or me or even Marie. I know she hated seeing me there last night. Maybe that's because she was afraid it would throw off her plan."

Meredith picked up her tea and sipped it. It was tepid, weak, and very sweet. "I understand you spent part of last night at your son's house." She paused. She thought she had heard a faint noise, like a muffled cry. "What was that?"

"What?"

"I thought I heard something." Meredith looked closely at Viola. "Mrs. Sumner, did you take Marie with you when you left last night? If you did, I could certainly understand it. You're her grandmother, and you're worried about her. But she's Lewis's child, and he has to be left to deal with her as best he can. If you've got Marie, he would be so relieved to see her. He's terribly upset."

Viola sat up straight. "Look, Ms. Whoever-You-Are. I'm sure you mean well, but I'm not some infant for you to chuck under the chin. Of course I don't have Marie, don't be ridiculous. If I took my granddaughter, as I have every right to do, I would say so, not sneak off, scaring everybody. You were asking me about last night. Well, I'll tell you. I was restless, my arm throbbed so, and I had a terrible headache. I just couldn't get comfortable in that house. Around three, I thought I heard somebody go downstairs. I had been wanting some warm milk, but I didn't want to risk running into Laura again. Once was enough, I promise you. It's terrible, the way she keeps an old woman from relaxing in her own son's house. Well, I waited a while, thinking maybe I'd go down after she came back up. I didn't hear her again, she seemed to be camped out down there, and I knew I couldn't sleep, so finally I just stepped back into my clothes and left. That was probably around four-thirty."

"When you left, did you hear or see Marie?"

"No, but that's not unusual. Lewis says she's a good little thing, she can sleep through a hurricane." Viola sniffed and dabbed her eyes.

"Did you see Laura?"

"No, but I rushed right out. I assure you."

Meredith paused again. She was sure she heard a small cry coming from the hallway. Abruptly, she stood and walked back down the passageway to a closed door she hadn't registered before.

"Mrs. Sumner, excuse me. Is this your restroom?"

"Don't go in there --."

Meredith turned the knob and pushed. The floor, constructed of minute white tiles stuck to blackened grout, dipped and cracked. A cheap, painted vanity with a chipped basin sat next to the toilet, and a pink gauze shower curtain stretched across the bathtub. Meredith grabbed hold of the curtain and yanked it aside. Behind

72

it, in the back corner near a frosted window, huddled a small, gray cat.

"I'm sorry. Please don't arrest me," Viola sniffed. "I got her from the shelter. I'm so lonely sometimes. I know I'm not supposed to have a pet in this apartment, but it's cruel, really. It's too quiet, just me and the television. What's an old lady supposed to do? I have to have someone to love, someone who needs me, even if it's just a pathetic little cat that nobody wants. And I thought Marie might like to play with her, when she comes for a visit. There's not a lot for her to do here, you see." Viola's tears spilled over. "I used to live in a nice house, with a garden and a piano, when my husband was alive and Lewis was home with me. Marie could have run around there, and I had neighbors that I liked. I told Laura I can still vacuum and carry out the trash. I'm really very strong, and Lewis could come once a week to cut the grass in the summertime, but she thought it was too much, and she didn't want Lewis to have the responsibility. She said she and Lewis needed to live their own lives, not be saddled with a dependent mother, so I couldn't move in with them either, but it wasn't reasonable. I'm sure I'd be a help. And it's not right. An old woman should be with her family. She should have her children and her grandchildren around her. I just wanted some company, that's all."

Meredith gently touched Viola's shoulder. "It's all right, Mrs. Sumner. She looks like a nice cat, and I'm sure you'll enjoy each other. But, do you have any other children to help you besides Lewis?"

"No, he's the only one. He does the best he can for me, under the circumstances. He's a good son. And I really am strong, I can still lift and haul and do the housework. I'm just lonely." She tugged a kleenex from the waistband of her skirt and wiped her nose with it.

"Yes, I see. I apologize for startling you. Thank you for your help. We're doing everything we can to find Marie. I'll be in touch."

Meredith hurried out the front door.

*

Five minutes south of Viola Sumner's, Meredith parked her car in front of another stubby apartment building. Its yard was several square feet of flattened grass, no bushes, no flowers, just a few coke cans tossed beside the cement walkway. Meredith shoved the outside door, which opened into a peeling vestibule. The scrawled label "Angelica Vasquez" was stuck next to a button with curling yellow tape. She pushed the button, and an answering buzzer unlatched the inner door.

Cautiously, Meredith climbed the dark wooden steps. It was suffocatingly hot. A baby cried, a jerky, breathless bleat. From the third floor landing, a chubby twentyish woman with black shoulder-length hair and heavy eye make-up peered over the railing.

"Oh. I was expecting my brother," she said with a slight, clicking accent.

"Sorry. My name is Meredith Bennett. I'm an attorney, helping the Sumners. Are you Angelica Vasquez?"

74

"No. I'm her sister Anita. Angelica, she is sick. She called them, I think. She went to the doctor." Anita eyed her suspiciously.

"Are you expecting her back soon?"

"No, not soon."

Clearly, Anita was not in an expansive mood. Meredith heard a shrill wail from inside the apartment. "Your children?" she asked.

"Yes."

It was hot in the hallway, and the cries grew louder. Meredith waited tensely on the top step. "Maybe we should check on them," she said finally.

Reluctantly, Anita admitted Meredith into the living room. Two small children, a boy and a girl, struggled on an old sofa covered with an orange sheet. The boy, the older of the two, waved a plastic doll over his head, out of his sister's reach. The girl was about three years old and completely bereft, her brown eyes overflowing with tears.

"Mi nina!" she cried.

"Luis, give her the doll. Que yo te dije?"

"Do you live here too?" Meredith asked Anita.

"No. Luis, para de luchar!"

"Well, if you don't mind my asking, what are you doing here?"

"We're family," Anita said shortly.

"Have you seen Angelica today?"

"Yes, for a minute, before she left." The girl's screams intensified. "Luis! Ahora! Juana, shhhh!"

"It's important that I talk to Angelica as soon as possible. Where is the doctor's office?"

Anita yanked Luis off the couch and grabbed the doll. "Mama, no!" he cried.

"I don't know if you'll catch her there. She might have gone someplace else."

"Please. It's important. I just need to talk with her. That's all."

"Okay. Maybe St. Francis, I don't know." Anita clamped the doll under her arm, and both children howled. "Shhh, los dije que se callaran!"

It was odd, Meredith thought, rushing down the stairs, that Anita and her children were visiting Angelica's apartment when Angelica was gone. It was probably just as she had said, some extended-family cultural difference. Maybe she should introduce Anita to Viola Sumner. She climbed back into her car and headed to St. Francis Hospital.

The St. Francis clinic waiting room was crowded with women and children who looked as if they had been forced to set up temporary camp there. Some of the kids wriggled on the floor to amuse themselves, while the sick ones drooped damply against their mothers' shoulders. The women chatted, pausing occasionally to scold in emphatic Spanish. Meredith stepped up to the receptionist's desk.

"Excuse me, I'm looking for a patient, Angelica Vasquez. It's very important. Is she here?"

The woman glanced at a scribbled list attached to a clipboard. "Catalina Diez," she called, and a short, round woman shot up from her chair and hurried through the door to the examining rooms. The telephone rang. "I think she was here earlier, but she's gone now." She picked up the phone.

"Are you sure?"

The receptionist waved at her and nodded as she listened to the caller. Finally, she hung up.

"When did she leave?"

"I don't know. She checked in late this morning, and I think she just saw the doctor a little while ago. You probably just missed her."

The phone jangled again, and a tired woman dragging a toddler approached the desk. "I'm sorry, but I have been waiting three hours. When is my turn?"

"Soon, it'll be soon."

"Did you notice if Angelica was alone?" Meredith asked. "Did she have a little girl with her?"

"Look, I'm busy. I don't notice these things. Excuse me." The receptionist picked up the phone and shrugged.

As soon as Meredith left the waiting room, a hunger pang stabbed her, and she realized that she had missed lunch. She bought a pack of orange peanut butter crackers and a diet coke at the hospital gift shop and perched on a couch under a palm frond in the lobby to rest. According to the hospital clock, it was already four. She would stop by the Sumners' to confer with Joe Field and then return home to reconnoiter with Maggie and Lucy after their scintillating afternoon with the cool Shawna. She felt a twinge of guilt when she thought of

Laura Sumner, waiting anxiously for her daughter to return while Meredith ran home to hers.

Meredith tossed the cellophane and brought her coke can back to the car. She imagined entering her empty house, work-related messages on the answering machine, and two hyper-chocolate-chipped children bounding up the walk and then relaxing into surliness in the security of her company. She would scramble eggs or boil hot dogs for dinner, and they would watch television in a hypnotized heap. Finally, bedtime would come, and she would tuck her daughters in and kiss them good night. Then she would soak in the bathtub or slide between the sheets with a cheap paperback.

How different it would be to come home to a kind, intelligent man, who would listen to her rehashes of the day's events and share the dishes and the children and the quiet hours ahead. Laura Sumner might read like a superwoman in the newspaper, but she was a fool. She had thrown away her husband and her child. If Meredith ever got a second chance at marriage, if she ever had a man like Lewis Sumner, she would make it last.

Chapter Ten

"That woman thinks I did it. You didn't hear her. I sold my soul to the law firm, I must be some cold bitch who could pitch her baby out the window from petty aggravation and then arrange it to look like a kidnapping. Yeah, well, what in the hell is she? And this torture I'm going through is just in my imagination, I'm such a damned great actress. I want my baby back, Lewis. I'm scared to death someone's hurting her." Laura's chest twisted, and she blocked the image. "I'm her mother. I love her." She wiped her nose. "Is that so damned hard to believe?"

It was Tuesday night. Marie had been missing less than twenty-four hours, but Laura's life had changed irrevocably. After Meredith Bennett had left that morning, Laura had ripped off her stockings and her suit and the white silk blouse and thrown the whole mess in the trash. Ms. Bennett had plodded out to do her witness interviews, and Lewis had followed the police to peek under porches, as if Marie were a stray cat. And Laura was supposed to stay in the house and wait for the phone to ring. She had thought that she was beyond that, waiting in the house while the men took care of important matters, and yesterday she would have been insulted and sarcastic, but today all she could manage was to sit here in optimistic horror. The men tried to make her think she was doing some kind of essential work, drooped cross-legged on the living room couch and crying her eyes out, but she knew they just wanted her out of the way. It was all she could do to keep breathing.

Lewis sat in the chair across from her. His face was gray with fatigue, his plastic frames skidding down his nose on a slick of oil and sweat. He looked defeated, too exhausted to push up his own glasses. But then, Laura thought, Lewis always looked like that. He probably hadn't eaten today because Angelica and his mother hadn't been around to stick food in front of him. Viola had called a couple of times, but she had soon gotten the message. Laura certainly couldn't be expected to comfort her mother-in-law today.

"Nobody thinks you hurt Marie," Lewis said quietly. "Meredith Bennett is an attorney, she has a job to do, she had to ask you a few questions. You of all people should understand that"

"So, now you're defending this woman against me. That's just great. You don't even know her, you didn't hear anything she said to me, but you automatically assume that she's right and I'm wrong. You know, you two would make a great couple, with your matching glasses and your twin airs of distracted incompetence. Maybe she should put me in jail with a couple of thugs and a piano wire, and then you two could get married and miraculously turn up Marie, who is probably sleeping peacefully in some cat box next to your mother's bed as we speak."

Lewis leaned back against the chair and closed his eyes. "I told you, Laura, my mother doesn't have Marie. She's an old lady. She's not going to pull a stunt like that."

"I'm tempted to believe you, you know. The one thing I've always been able to count on is your superficial honesty. But Viola hates me, she would do anything to beat me. And together, you've always made quite a team, devoted daddy and granny saving baby from the big bad wolf. But I never imagined you'd go this far. Well, you win. I give up. Just have your mother produce Marie, and we'll all pretend you had nothing to do with it. We'll go back to the beginning." Laura shifted forward and stared intensely, willing Lewis's eyes to hers. Tears rushed down her face. "Please, Lewis, I can't stand this. I can't stand the thought that some lunatic might be hurting my little girl, and there's not a thing I can do to help her."

Lewis stood up from the chair and sat next to his wife on the couch. He took her limp hand between his two warm ones. "I know, Laura. I wish I could bring Marie back. I wish I could make everything all right. But I feel the same way you do, just the same. I don't know where she is, and I'm terrified. But the police will do everything they can. We just have to believe that."

Laura yanked her hand away and stood up. "I'm going to check my messages."

Richard would have grabbed her. He would have pushed her back onto the couch and said, "You're not checking any damn messages," which he would know she didn't care about in the least, and then he would have held her and shaken her or kissed her hard, a bruising, angry kiss that would have ground her lips against his teeth. She needed his power and relentlessness, the feeling that she had met her match. Lewis quietly returned to his chair. She could squash him with a word. He was contemptible.

She picked up the phone and punched in her voice mail number. Richard had left several short messages expressing his concern. She wanted to go upstairs to call him, but she couldn't use her bedroom phone. She could not walk by Marie's empty bedroom, its windows now tightly closed and locked. Laura went into the kitchen and dialed his home number. She just had to hope that Lewis would not come in. This was not a good time for him to discover her relationship with Richard.

"Orwell," he answered. Laura could picture him posed in his marble foyer, his hip grazing the ebony Steinway beneath the stairs, the black telephone receiver pushed to his ear. He would have been lounging in the study, listening to Bach as he orchestrated the destruction of his opponents, and sipping tonic water with a twist.

"It's me."

"Darling, at last, thank goodness. I was so worried about you. Have they found Marie?"

"No." She began to weep. "Richard, this is the most terrible thing. I love her so much. What if, what if...." She was sobbing now.

"Is Lewis there with you?"

"Yes, he's here, we're alone now, it's awful. He's trying to be nice, I suppose, he's just being himself, but I can't stand it. He brings out the worst in me, the very rock bottom. This is just too much for me. I don't know what to do. Someone could be hurting Marie right now, frightening her, torturing her...." Laura was crying hysterically. Lewis came into the kitchen. Immediately, she stiffened.

"Hang on," she said to Richard. She placed her palm over the receiver. "What do you want?"

"I think you should say good-bye now. You need to take some valium and try to get some rest. This isn't helping anyone. Besides, we should keep the line clear in case there's any news."

"All right. You just get out of here, and I'll finish." Lewis nodded and left the kitchen. She heard his footsteps ascending the stairs.

"I'm sorry. I have to go. I have to keep the line clear."

"Laura, listen to me. I want you to get in your car and drive over here. You're just making yourself miserable, staying there with him. Lewis can mind the phone. You come here, you can sleep in my bed -- our bed. I'll help you, Darling. There's no reason for you to stay in that house a minute longer."

Laura could see Richard, his face flushed with the passion of his argument, his long, slim figure bent persuasively, his fingers combing through his hair as he brushed away distractions. It would be wonderful to be with him. He would protect her, and she might be able to sleep. But she couldn't leave. Marie would expect her to be here. She needed to be here in case Marie came back.

"Richard, I can't. You're wonderful, and I love you, but I have to stay here in case Marie comes home."

"Very well, Laura," he said coldly. "Stay with your husband tonight. Perhaps it would be best. Are you sure you're safe in that house?"

"Yes. I'm sure. Don't frighten me. I'll be perfectly fine. The windows are locked, and Lewis is here."

"If you're sure."

"Yes, I'm sure. I love you," she said.

"I love you," Richard replied.

Laura put down the phone. Lewis was standing in the doorway. She hadn't heard him come down the stairs.

By midnight, Angelica had lain on a narrow bed in the St. Francis emergency room for three hours. Blue curtains surrounded her small private space, and hoses and nozzles protruded from the wall behind her. She had draped her shorts over the back of a metal chair and wadded her rinsed panties in a clump of paper towels on the seat. A paper sheet covered her naked hips, and a plastic-backed pad beneath her soaked up the blood. It was hard to stay awake and hard to sleep. She shivered and shifted her sticky legs.

"I'm sorry your doctor is taking so long." A bearded young man came in. He was wearing a uniform, a blue cotton shirt and matching pants, the same fabric as the curtains. "He's performing an emergency c-section. He told me to start an I.V. Are you hemorrhaging?

"I don't know. I'm bleeding."

He swabbed a blue vein in Angelica's left hand. "This is going to hurt for a minute."

She looked away. The needle pierced her skin and slid into the vein, an eerie sting. He taped over the spot where the needle entered her body. A clear tube led to a plastic bag dangling from a pole.

"Just glucose for now. The doctor wants us to be ready, in case you need a D&C. Nothing to worry about." He patted her arm and left.

A few minutes later, a pretty young woman in a white coat and flowered dress and a tag reading, "Dr. Kimberley," pushed back the curtain. "How are you doing?" she asked.

"I'm okay."

"Are you having a lot of bleeding?"

"It goes drip, drip, drip, every second, and I got worried. The doctor said to come here."

"When did the bleeding start?"

"A few days ago. The doctor, he said I would lose the baby, but I could probably manage alone. But, tonight, the bleeding is too much."

"How far along were you?"

"Ten weeks. Only ten weeks."

"A lot of miscarriages occur in the first trimester of pregnancy. There was probably something wrong with the way the baby was developing, and your body took care of it. I know it must be difficult, but it's probably for the best."

"Yes." Angelica bit her lip and touched the silver cross lying askew on her chest.

"This pad is soaked, but I don't think you're hemorrhaging. Has the embryo come out yet?"

"I don't know."

"It would be a firm, grayish mass. I see clots, but I don't see the embryo here. I'll have the nurse get you a clean pad, and I'm hoping your doctor will be here soon. Do you want a blanket?"

"Yes, please."

The man in the blue uniform came in and covered her with a blanket, a cocoon of cotton and blood. She closed her eyes, and Marie, in a summer dress, danced before them.

"I'm sorry to keep you waiting like this." It was her doctor. "I'm going to give you pitocin through your I.V. It will increase your cramping, and hopefully, you'll be able to expel the embryonic material on your own. Otherwise, we'll do a D&C tomorrow. I'm going to admit you to the hospital overnight. Is there anyone you want to call?"

"Yes, my sister."

"The nurse will take you to a phone, and then up to your room. See you in the morning. Oh, and don't worry. This is very common. In all likelihood, you will have no trouble with your next pregnancy."

The man in the blue uniform brought Angelica a hospital gown. That doctor knew nothing. She had had three miscarriages, and she would never go through this misery again, never. She wiped her nose with the back of her hand.

"What time is it?" she asked the man, when he wheeled her to a telephone.

"Two-fifteen," he said.

"Thank you, I won't call my sister now. I'll call in the morning."

Anita would surely be asleep by now, and she didn't want to wake the children. She would have to remember to call Lewis in the morning too. She would tell him she had the flu, and she needed a few days off.

*

Mike Ramsey shivered. It was a warm July night, really early morning now, but the wind off the lake chilled his sweaty arms. He did not want to walk the ten blocks to the beach lugging the heavy trash bag, but he had no choice. He couldn't bury it in his backyard. That was the first place the police would look, once they suspected him.

He had to hope that no one noticed him. The houses on Cherry were dark, just a few odd lights in children's bedrooms. Even the Sumners' house was dark. And for all her talk of being a light sleeper, his mother had not heard him leave. That was lucky, because he didn't know what he would have told her about the bag.

He passed the playground, through the trees, toward the enormous stairway, where the grassy park ended abruptly in a cliff. A scrap of sand and the dark lake, an endless blot, lay below. He hurried down the steps, twenty, thirty, gripping the heavy bag in one hand and the grimy metal rail in the other.

He picked a place under the foot of the stairs, where children would be less likely to dig. Then he reached into the bag and pulled out the shovel his mother used to plant tulip bulbs. It was small, but it seemed sturdy. He had forgotten how noisy the lake could be. Sometimes it was peaceful, like gently rippling glass, but now white-tipped waves boomed against the beach. Once he had loved to play in the waves, to jump over them or to let them wash over his head, when he could escape his mother's grasp for just an afternoon.

The hole was deep, but the bag was bulky, and he had to be sure that no one would find it. He should take the time to dig a larger hole, but he was frightened. If someone came now, he would be finished. But no one would come at four o'clock in the morning. He had to calm down.

The shovel was too small, this was taking too long. Mike threw it aside and began to scratch with his fingers, scooping out handfuls of sand and dirt. The cool wind lashed his damp skin, and the sky was brightening. He had to finish quickly, or someone would catch him. He thrust the bag into the hole, flattened the black plastic and pushed the dirt and sand over it. He stuck the shovel in his back jeans pocket, wiped his hands on his legs, and rushed back up the stairs.

Chapter Eleven

On Wednesday afternoon, the day after Marie's disappearance, Meredith perched on the edge of a chair opposite Lewis and Laura, who sat at opposite ends of their white couch with their legs crossed away from each other. Laura wore the same baggy gray shorts and crumpled tee shirt as yesterday, and her arms and legs protruded from her clothes like popsicle sticks. Lewis, neat in khaki slacks and a plaid sport shirt, listened to Meredith attentively and asked appropriate questions. Only the dark smears under his eyes and his concerted evenness betrayed his distress.

"We've looked under every porch and shrub and sandbox lid within two miles of this house, and we still haven't found Marie," he said. "Did the police talk to our neighbors?"

"Yes, but I'm afraid the results were disappointing," Meredith responded.

While listening to Lewis, she had decided to be straightforward. He was thinking clearly, he wanted to know the truth, and she thought he could handle it. And since he was bright and concerned and knew the key players and the territory well, he might also be able to provide her with some valuable insights. Still, there was no reason to slap him with difficult news. She would be honest, but she would try to ease into it.

"The kidnapping probably occurred in the early morning hours, possibly around three, when Laura heard Marie cry and your mother heard someone go downstairs. Meredith glanced at Laura, who withdrew deeper into the couch. "At that hour, your neighbors were sleeping. Most of them have air conditioning, at least in the adult bedrooms, so that their windows were closed, some with the additional noise of window units. We were hoping for one sleepless person, a mother walking a restless baby, somebody, but we had no luck."

"So, what happens now?"

"Well, I pushed the lab to hurry with the hair and fingerprint samples the police took from Marie's bedroom. According to their preliminary findings, several of the hairs are consistent with the curl from Marie's baby book. Two appear to be Laura's, and two are yours. The last three black hairs do not seem to belong to a family member. The fingerprints are yours and Laura's, and again, an unidentified set."

"They're probably Angelica's," said Lewis.

"I think you're right. We'll find out today. I visited her this morning at the hospital. She seemed pretty upset about the whole thing, and she gave me her fingerprints and a hair sample. She certainly has black hair, and the lab said that, just eyeballing them, the prints did appear to be a match."

Laura looked up and cleared her throat. "Well, I think it's quite a coincidence that she turns up sick on the same day that Marie disappears. What's wrong with her, anyway?"

"I told you, she's got the flu," Lewis said.

"Yeah, you told me all right." She turned to Meredith. "So, how do you know this woman you talked to in the hospital is even Angelica? These people have enormous families, sisters coming out of the woodwork. Anyone of them could have played her part. And how many Angelica Vasquez's do you think there are in this city? She practically could have bet there'd be one in the hospital somewhere, just by the sheer operation of chance. I'll bet Angelica ran into financial trouble and decided to sell Marie. They're both probably hundreds of miles from here by now."

Meredith squeezed her pen. "I called her apartment this morning, and her sister Anita told me to go to the hospital. I got her room number from St. Francis information. Her name was written on the blackboard in the hall near her room. She knew your family. I know you're under a lot of strain, Mrs. Sumner, but just because I am a public servant instead of a partner in a fancy law firm doesn't mean that I can't do my job."

Laura sat up straight. She unfurled one arm and pointed a thin finger at Meredith. "Look, Lady, you're way out of line. You know nothing about what I'm going through. There is nothing personal going on here. We are not friends. This is a professional relationship, and you work for me, and I have every right to ask you pertinent questions. Lewis is allowed to, isn't he, without getting in trouble? Oh, but I forgot. He's such a nice guy."

"That's enough, Laura," Lewis said tightly.

"Oh, this is sweet. I hardly recognized you in your shining armor. Should I leave so you two can continue chatting cozily about the kidnapping of my daughter?" She turned back to Meredith. "So, what in the hell did Angelica say?"

"I talked to her for about an hour." Meredith straightened her back. She had been wrong to attack Laura, however disagreeable she was. Laura did have every right to question every step of this investigation. If Lucy were missing, she would do the same thing. "She had spent most of last night in the emergency room."

Meredith remembered how exhausted Angelica had been, the I.V. tubing attached to her hand waving wanly with her weak gestures. When Meredith told her that Marie was missing, and that someone might have kidnapped her, Angelica crossed herself and began to sob. That was when she told Meredith about her miscarriage. "I have lost all my children," she sniffed. "Please don't tell Mr. Lewis and Mrs. Laura. They won't like it, they won't understand. I am not married. Please."

"Angelica said she was sick in bed Monday night, and she spent yesterday at the doctor's. Last night she felt worse and came to the emergency room, and they admitted her."

"So, what's wrong with her?"

"Female troubles," Meredith supplied abruptly. "She should be going home this afternoon."

Lewis blushed. Meredith felt a rush of warmth for him. He was in the same situation as Laura, but he handled it so differently.

"To continue," she said, focusing on Lewis's eyes, "the only fingerprints on the ladder are your painter

Mike Ramsey's. There aren't any footprints below the window, since the weather has been so dry." She paused, regauging his mental state, and then rushed forward. "The police found no traces of blood in the bedroom, the hallway, on the ladder, or on Mike's work knife, which was apparently used to cut the screen." Lewis squinted, as if in pain, and Meredith waited until he nodded to her to proceed. "The kidnapper exhibited knowledge of Marie's location in the house, and, as you pointed out, he allowed her to take her favorite blanket. Is Marie afraid of strangers?"

"Not particularly," said Lewis. "She has four caretakers, counting my mother, and they have all been good to her. I think she expects the best of people."

"Would she cry if a stranger picked her up?"

"Maybe a whimper, if he woke her, but not afterwards. She is a very good-natured child."

"Or a dead one," said Laura. They looked at her. "Well, if she were dead, she wouldn't have cried either."

"I think the fact that her blanket is missing is a hopeful sign," said Meredith.

"Perhaps. Perhaps not. There's no need to be a pansy about this. It's not as if the possibility isn't with us every single moment. She could be dead, couldn't she? And maybe that would be better, compared to what else could be happening to her right now." She grasped both her arms and looked up belligerently. "Unless your boyfriend Lewis here took her to hide her from me, which I'm sure is beyond the realm of possibility. He's much too sweet a person." Laura grimaced at Lewis, who lowered his eyes.

Meredith inhaled. She was not going to let Laura goad her again. Laura was distraught. And it was going to be worse in a moment.

"I need to tell you something else our investigation has uncovered. Somehow, the media has obtained this information, and I don't want you to be surprised. We did background checks on Angelica and Mike Ramsey. Angelica checked out fine, no criminal record. Maybe you checked before you hired her, and you know that already. Mike, on the other hand, did some time in juvenile detention a couple of years ago."

"What did he do?" asked Lewis.

"He molested a six-year-old girl."

"Oh my God." Laura started to cry. Lewis put his head in his hands.

"The police picked him up early this morning and questioned him for quite a long time. He says he didn't take Marie, and we have no evidence that he did."

"But it all fits, doesn't it?" said Laura.

"It fits, but it's not the only thing that fits. We told him not to leave town."

"I can't believe he'd do it," murmured Lewis. "He seems like such an unassuming guy. And his poor mother, what she must be going through. Her husband died a few years ago, and she's had to raise the boy alone."

"Christ, what are you, some kind of saint, or just plain stupid? That woman raised some creep who probably did unspeakable things to your daughter. They both make me sick, and so do you, if you're sticking up for them." Laura swiveled wildly toward Meredith. "I

94

can't stand this anymore. You can't do your job right because you've got a thing for my husband, don't deny it, I know the signs, and he's worried about our buddy the child molester's mother. Has everybody gone nuts?" She leaped to her feet and ran upstairs. Meredith heard a door slam.

"I'm sorry," Meredith said. "But I'm sure you understand. We need proof that he did something in this particular case. And frankly, I hope we don't find it. I know that a lot of people love Marie, and I still think it is quite possible that she is well and happy somewhere else."

"That's one of the many things that makes living with that woman so damned difficult," said Lewis. "I still think she may be doing an incredible job of putting us all on."

Carolyn Ramsey sat in the kitchen wondering if she dared sneak into her own living room to dust the coffee table. Even from here, she could detect a faint commotion, no discernable words, but definite voices instead of the usual silence. Thank goodness she had drawn the sheers this morning to protect her furniture from fading, though she had left the front windows open a few inches, a chink in her armor. But it was so hot, she had to have some air. Even a captured ladybug got a few holes punched in the lid of her jar.

Carolyn had spent the last four years lying to her neighbors. Now it was over. Mike had been a child himself, he had touched a little girl, he did wrong, and he had paid for it. But, where was the justice? They didn't send sixteen-year-old Johnny Fairchild to jail for knocking up his girlfriend in the backseat of the family Volvo. Susie Manilow just had an abortion, and that wasn't a crime either, just good practical thinking. Frederick Marshall divorced his wife, who had cared for him and their five children for twenty years, to marry a blonde executive fifteen years his junior. But that was natural male behavior, and Fred had money and position. He could be forgiven his foibles. But not Mike. Mike was a middle-class only child with a dead father, and nobody was going to cut him an inch of slack for a mistake he made when he was just a kid. They were going to rub his face in the muck and then hang him from the old oak tree.

Well, to hell with them. Carolyn thought, they're not going to keep me prisoner in my kitchen. She reached under the sink for a clean rag and a bottle of lemon oil and then crept down the hall, tiptoeing from shadow to shadow, avoiding the streaks of sunshine. She slid into the living room, up against the drapes. The voices, clear now, seeped through the open window.

"And what is your reaction to the news that you are living on the same block as a convicted child molester?"

"I'm horrified. I moved here because it seemed to be a nice, safe place to raise my children, and now I hear this. At least someone should have warned us, given us some kind of notice about this guy, so we could take precautions. My kids walk home from school past his house everyday. For all I know, he's been watching them out the window all this time. It's enough to make your skin crawl. And now poor little Marie Sumner is gone, and nobody's even arresting him. He's still in that house, posing a threat to every innocent child in the area."

Carolyn peeked around the drapes and through the sheers. A reporter standing on the sidewalk held a microphone toward Julie Ellis from two doors down. Julie Ellis didn't know where her children were unless they were home in bed at night. She spent her days playing tennis, shopping, and eating lunch, while some underpaid illegal alien scrubbed her floor and drove her children from day camp to karate class to a fast food restaurant for chicken blobs and plastic toys. Her children would probably turn out just like Frederick Marshall, committing heartless crimes the legal way. And Julie Ellis would be proud of them for it. They would be American success stories.

"Hi, Mom." Mike slunk in, fresh from a mid-day shower.

"Shhh, stay back!" Carolyn gestured frantically.

A group of women huddled in a tight clutch on the parkway. A few stragglers joined them, and they whispered and pointed indignantly at the house. The T.V. camera was taping them. It would be all over the news tonight.

Two police cars pulled up.

"Mike, go upstairs, quickly."

Carolyn had spent her whole adult life caring for Mike. She had washed his skinned knees and cooked his vegetables and sewn his Indian costumes and searched for the right plastic machine gun. She had been father and mother to him when Jack was too busy or sick or dead. She wasn't going to stop taking care of him now, when he needed her most.

The doorbell rang. She set the lemon oil and rag on the piano bench, smoothed her hair and skirt, and went to the door.

"Who is it?" she asked shrilly.

"Police." Carolyn opened the door.

"Officer, thank heavens you're here. These people are harassing us and trespassing on our property."

"I'm sorry, Ma'am, but we're here to search your house and grounds." He thrust a document in her face.

"What on earth are you looking for?"

"Mrs. Ramsey, I think you'd better sit down with a magazine. This may take a while."

Carolyn went back to the kitchen. She could hear the police turning out drawers and moving furniture. She stared out the back window. Two officers were digging in the back garden. Mike came downstairs and sat quietly with her at the kitchen table. His face was white, and his knees were shaking. She wanted to put her arms around him, but she couldn't. She couldn't touch him. God deliver us, she prayed, from this unbelievable horror.

Chapter Twelve

It was night. Lewis stood in Marie's doorway. The teddy bears danced in darkness, a mocking frolic. The windows were closed and locked. Locking the barn door after the horse escaped, better late than never, all's well that end's well. Lewis's brain whirred with his mother's useless aphorisms. The police had taken the screen as evidence, and Lewis didn't want any living creature entering through that window again. Better safe than sorry.

He had to figure this out. Marie could be out there somewhere, needing him, crying for him, waiting for her daddy to rescue her. Meredith and the police might come up with something, he knew they were trying, but nobody loved Marie like he did, nobody else would try so hard. And he was smarter than they were, and more familiar with the situation. His mind buzzed with the facts that he knew and the probabilities of certain events. He had to think. Marie needed him, and nobody else seemed to be doing a damn thing, just little plodding tippy-toe steps while she could be suffering, her time could be running out.

According to one theory, someone had carried the heavy ladder that lay in Lewis's backyard thirty feet to Marie's window. He had climbed the ladder, used Mike's knife to cut the screen, and slid in through the opening. Once he had Marie, he had climbed back down with her and replaced the ladder. Possible, but a cumbersome job at best. Unless the kidnapper had a key to the house.

The back door was locked and latched from the inside when Lewis came downstairs, so the kidnapper couldn't have entered or exited that way. The front door had locked automatically, but the deadbolt was open. Lewis routinely bolted the doors before he went to bed, and he thought he had done it on Monday night, but he couldn't exactly remember. To enter or leave through the front door, the kidnapper must have had a key to the house. As far as he knew, only four people had keys, and three of them were already inside.

He knew that he and his mother hadn't taken Marie. His mother had heard footsteps at around three a.m. If that were Laura leaving, she would have had a good three hours to take Marie to a prearranged location and return home. It was possible, but, he conceded, unlikely. Laura was cunning, but she was doing an awfully good job of simulating hysteria.

Angelica also had a key. But caring for Marie was her job, she did it for money. He supposed she might have taken Marie to sell her, but it was hard to imagine the little housekeeper taking that much initiative or behaving so callously. Besides, she was sick, she had even been hospitalized.

Of course, there could be more than four keys. Laura might have given a copy of her key to anyone. Which brought him inevitably to Richard Orwell.

Lewis entered Laura's room. She was asleep in her clothes on top of the bedspread. For the last few nights, she had slept in the evening, when Lewis was awake. Around eleven, she would wake up and wander restlessly around the house or sit on the living room couch with her feet tucked under her and stare. After Meredith left this afternoon, he had convinced Laura to take a shower, but she had automatically retrieved the same rumpled clothes from the bathroom floor and stepped back into them. Now she lay pale and tousled on her side, her knees pulled close to her chest.

"Laura?" He tapped her shoulder. She sat up straight, her eyes wide and smeary. "I've been thinking. Did you ever give our house key to anyone?"

"What do you mean?"

"I mean, did you give a key to our house to Richard Orwell?"

"Why would I do that?" She looked up at Lewis sneakily. He wanted to punch her.

"Look, Laura. Despite what you may think of me, I am not a stupid man. You just think about that. You just think about how long it takes a reasonably intelligent person to read a neon billboard. You think about the facts and our life together and how much I must know and how long I've known it, before you start playing coy with me."

Laura backed up against the headboard and crossed her arms over her chest. "What are you talking about?" Maybe he should have done this a long time ago. She actually sounded scared. It was exhilarating.

"I'm talking about you and Richard. Our marriage is gone, it's dead. We might as well get this out on the table. I know about you and Richard and your affair. I know you've been trying to keep it a secret so the custody judge won't call you what you are, an unfit mother, and who knows what they might think at the almighty office about a partner and his eager pupil, never mind about me. Well, I'll tell you something that may surprise you. Richard did me a favor, a damn big one. You think we don't know each other, a nodding acquaintance, a business call passed on to you. That shows how clever and sensitive you are, Lady. That's fine. You cling to your illusions. But I need to know -- does Richard Orwell have a key to this house?"

"How long have you known about Richard and me?"

"I've known for two years. Two years of your changing phones and murmuring into the receiver, two years of your late meetings and business trips. You think I'm too much of a dope to notice. Well, I didn't notice at first. I trusted you. But then I talked to Richard."

"You talked to him?"

"All that lurking in dark corners and fibbing to hubby was just for your titillation, My Dear. Richard thought you would enjoy a little romantic deception, and he was right. Only it was you that got fooled. Big, tough Laura, the macho man. You've been the pawn of men all along."

"Do you mean you talked to Richard and went along with our relationship? I don't understand."

"I think I've told you enough. Now, what about the key?"

Laura stood up. Her knees wobbled. "I'm getting out of here. You're crazy. You don't know what you're saying."

Lewis grabbed her shoulders and shook her. She was so frail, her body moved like a leaf in the wind. "Laura, damn it, does Richard Orwell have a key to this house?"

"Yes, yes he does. So what? He gave me his, so I gave him mine. What do you care?"

Lewis released her. She ran down the stairs and out the front door. It dangled open behind her like a broken habit.

Meredith leaned over the coffee table and spread Deadly Red enamel on her big toenail. The window fan blew her nightgown up around her thighs. Maggie, a perfectionist, had snuggled a cotton ball between each of her own toes. Her shiny red ellipses fanned elegantly next to Meredith's scrunched ones. Lucy, the eight-year-old, swung her arms in a demented windmill to dry her fingernails. As she strutted around the living room, fibers of gold shag carpet clung to her damp toes. Meredith noticed and frowned. But she hated the carpet, and Lucy must live with her own furry toes, the result of her carelessness.

Meredith screwed the cap back on the polish and returned it to Maggie. "All right, time for bed."

"Do we have to? I'm not tired. I can never sleep anyway," Lucy complained, as Maggie plucked the balls from between her toes and left them strewn around the coffee table.

"You have to. Maggie, the cotton, please." Scampering, Lucy kicked up her skinny legs under one of Alexander's old White Sox tee shirts, while Maggie laboriously collected cotton balls. "Take a cool shower and wet your hair, and you'll be more comfortable in bed. When the fan blows, it'll work just like an air conditioner."

"Do we have to?"

"No. I just thought it might make you feel better. Now, give me a kiss, and off you go."

Each girl gravely presented her mouth to her mother. Meredith knew they would stay up together for an hour or so, and she would try to ignore the giggles and thuds. They weren't tired quite yet, but she was. She needed some time to be, not a prosecutor or a mother, but just to be.

She picked up her iced tea glass and wandered into the kitchen. Glimpsing her reflection in the upper oven door, she fluffed her brown hair and touched her jaw line. Meredith thought of Lewis Sumner, sick with despair over his missing daughter and chained to his overbearing wife. Laura and Lewis were probably fighting right now, Laura attacking, Lewis conciliatory. Meredith's sympathies lay completely with Lewis. The fact that he hadn't murdered Laura in all these years demonstrated incredible self-restraint in the face of overwhelming provocation.

She carried her refilled iced tea back to the couch and plopped in front of the fan. Dr. Alexander, sealed in his Kenilworth meat locker, would never appreciate this small pleasure. Just as he had failed to appreciate her unbleached, Estee Lauderless charms, she thought. At best she had worn thin, as real people will when compared with the "Sports Illustrated" swimsuit issue. She rested the icy glass against her neck. She might have afforded a couple of window units, but she didn't want them. There must be some time of year when a person could exist in the air, like a living animal in nature instead of a chicken leg.

She closed her eyes. The warm breeze, gentle fingers through her hair, caressed her face and moved her nightgown over her breasts. Then Maggie laughed, a free, irrepressible release. She wished she had that with someone, some easy time to laugh and touch and just be. She didn't need a man to take care of her or to prove her worth. She just missed that kind of love.

Once she and Alexander had had it. In their tiny apartment, he had lifted her through the air, her naked legs around his waist, to drop enraptured onto the nearest flat surface. That intensity couldn't last forever, but some spark of it could. In a good marriage, after the trials of work and groceries and whining children, that spark could still be fanned into a flame. But Alexander hadn't the patience, and his eye had flickered instead to the nearest shiny object. The sad part was that, for Meredith, the spark was still there. In anger and despair, she had buried it, but sometimes, as now, when she was alone at night, she could still feel the tickle of its heat.

She thought again of Lewis Sumner. With his thick glasses and receding hair, he was hardly a pin-up. But he was bright and kind and patient, and if he loved you, it would mean something. After the wound Alexander had inflicted, Lewis's sort of dependability and devotion were very attractive. Poor guy. He was hardly in a state for romance at the moment. Meredith opened her eyes and sighed and scrounged under the couch for the remote control. She would watch a few minutes of television, anything, just to distract herself. Then she would take a shower and go to bed. Tomorrow she would see Lewis again.

Chapter Thirteen

At nine a.m., Meredith rang the Sumners' back doorbell. She had taken some care with her appearance, a pale blue belted cotton dress open at the collar, pink lipstick, and bare white sandals revealing her fancy toes. It was too hot for stockings, and her legs were still good, in spite of Maggie and Lucy. She had showered again this morning, and her clean hair fluffed against her cheeks.

"Hello." Lewis smiled slightly and admitted her to the kitchen. He looked tired. He had been eating cinnamon toast and orange juice, like a child.

"Any word yet?"

"No. I'm sorry."

"I've had three calls from reporters already this morning. Now that they've heard about Mike Ramsey, they all want interviews. I hate those people. They make everyone look cheap."

"I know," Meredith paused. "But I think you should seriously consider talking to them. They could be useful. It's time for you and Laura to go on T.V., if you can face it, and make a plea for Marie's safe return. We can call a press conference, really, the sooner the better. Maybe somebody knows something and just hasn't focused on the situation."

"I think that's fine, but Laura isn't here." Lewis turned to the counter and started fussing with the coffeemaker. Then he swiveled back and looked Meredith straight in the face. "We had an argument last night, you know how she is, and she stormed out, and she never came back."

Meredith heard a soft shuffle, and then the basement door pushed open. Meredith hadn't noticed it before. Lewis's mother, Viola, emerged. "Hello, Dear," she said. "Just doing a little housework. Any news of Marie?"

"No. I'm sorry."

"Oh, dear. We do miss her so, and now that man -- it's so frightening." Her eyes were red and puffy.

"That's all right, Mother. You go sit in the living room and rest, and let me talk to Meredith for a minute."

"All right, Son. I am a bit tired." Viola walked into the living room. Lewis shut the door behind her.

"Do you have any idea where Laura might be?" Meredith asked him.

"Oh, yeah, I have a good idea. I thought Laura would tell you the truth, I hoped she would, but I don't think she did. She does have a boyfriend. Richard Orwell is his name. He's one of her partners. I knew about their affair, but I didn't know until last night that he has a key to this house. I think he might have taken Marie, with or without Laura's help, and Laura might have gone to him so that they could be a family, the three of them. I think this whole thing was some kind of wild scheme so that they could be together with no interference from me."

"But those two are experts at using the legal system to their advantage. Why would they commit a felony to avoid a custody hearing? And they couldn't keep Marie's presence a secret for long. I can't believe Laura would risk her career and her freedom in order to avoid a court battle. From what I can see, she thrives on battles."

"Maybe she figures there's not much of a risk. They'll just disappear, move to some state where nobody knows them. They've got plenty of money -- you wouldn't believe the amount of money those two make. Richard knew that Laura was staying here with me in order to be with Marie. Maybe he couldn't stand the wait anymore, and he realized that the only way he could have Laura to himself was if he also had Marie. Or maybe he thought that Marie would always be in the way, between him and Laura, and he decided to get rid of her for good."

Meredith walked toward Richard Orwell's Gold Coast townhouse. She had driven to his office first, where he surely should have been at ten on a Thursday morning, but his secretary would only say that he hadn't arrived yet, and she would be happy to give him a message. After several minutes of hunting, Meredith had spotted a metered parking space a few blocks west of Richard's address, on a broad, naked avenue studded with apartment buildings and convenience stores. His street was narrow and charming, with tree-lined sidewalks and gracious brick homes, beveled glass and ivy. Tiny front yards displayed carefully groomed grass, and window boxes sprouted perfect assortments of flowers and trailing greenery. Meredith approached the gray stone townhouse, its granite surfaces creating a sense of solidity and tradition. She rang the bell. She waited and rang again. No one answered.

From a pay phone, Meredith dialed Richard's home, where an answering machine picked up after two rings. Then she called his secretary, who said that she hadn't realized that Meredith was going to start searching for Richard all over town, that he had gone to New York yesterday, and he wasn't scheduled to return until tomorrow. Meredith insisted on obtaining his client's office number in New York. She called and was told that Richard had completed his business yesterday afternoon. The client did not know whether Richard had stayed in New York last night or returned to Chicago immediately.

*

Katie Tyler had wanted rollerblades for as long as she could remember. After much begging and promising, yes, she really would use them, no, she wouldn't break every bone in her body, her parents had finally come through yesterday, for her eleventh birthday. Katie's mother had insisted that she wear knee pads, black blobs adhering to her legs like leeches, and a helmet that plastered her hair to her head and retained all of her body heat. Katie had imagined herself flying free along the sidewalk, the wind filling her thick hair like a sail. Instead, she was sweating shamefully as she struggled to keep up with the accomplished Erin Weissman, who was probably in Wisconsin by now.

"Hey, Erin, wait up." Katie shouted, skidding nervously along the bike path, her head a boiled egg in its plastic shell.

She struggled past the train station, its tracks running parallel to the bike path all the way to Kenosha. A young man waiting for the 9:50 to Chicago watched her troubled progress and snickered when her feet drifted and she had to wave her arms to stay upright.

"On your left!"

A biker whizzed past. Startled, Katie tripped and hurtled forward. She only had time to panic, to wish herself upright and wonder what to do, before her knees slammed the path. But her torso continued relentlessly, smashing her chin on the asphalt.

She lay on the path in shock, her stomach flopping like a fish. Gradually, she assessed the physical damage. The pads had saved her knees, and some of the skin was scraped from her palms, but the worst was her chin. She was afraid it might have shattered. A wave of nausea curled from her tummy to her back. She rested her head on the path.

It's okay, she promised herself, I'm okay. Slowly, she sat, then worked up the nerve to touch her chin. It felt like a raw, hard knob, but it wasn't dripping blood, just hugely swollen, and the bone underneath seemed solid. She would be all right. But she was shaking, and she was afraid of falling again. She could not skate home. She would have to take off her skates and walk home in her socks. She hoped the young man had caught his train by now, though she hadn't heard one pass. She must look terrible, with a gigantic, blue chin and grubby tear streaks on her cheeks.

Katie reached down to untie her laces. Drat! One of the wheels was missing from the bottom of her right skate. Maybe she had smashed it down at a funny angle when she fell, and the wheel had broken off and rolled away, or maybe the wheel just fell off by itself, and that's why she lost her balance. In any case, these skates were probably defective and could be returned to the store for a full refund or exchanged for something better, like a board game. Katie wasn't sure if her mother would need the missing wheel to return the skates, but she might. She peered up and down the path, but she couldn't spot it.

She laid her skates on the gravel edging the path. Scattered weeds grew along the fence on the train tracks side, and she picked through those first in a vain search for the small disc. The east side was wider, a scruffy forest, thin trees and tall grass and wildflowers. The wheel could be hiding under a leaf or stuck in a clot of browning roots. But she had to search. Her mother would ask her if she had tried.

The tall grass crunched under her feet, and Katie was grateful for her thick white socks. She crouched and felt the ground in a two-foot strip along the path. The forest sloped gently downward, and Katie realized that the wheel might have rolled some distance before it finally stopped in a tangle of plants. She couldn't search the whole area. It was too densely covered, and her chances of success were small. Perhaps it wasn't worth the trouble. Her mother could surely return the skates without the wheel. Katie turned to leave. She would pick up her skates and stumble home. Erin would find her there eventually.

As she turned back toward the path, Katie's eyes passed over the wooded area twenty feet ahead of her and just at the bottom of the slope. She thought she saw something. It wasn't the black wheel. It was a patch of white, a large patch, about two feet square. It lay several inches above the earth, but below the seedy grass tops and the still, lacey flowers. Perhaps it was a towel flung from a biker's sweaty neck or a piece of scrap paper swept up from the residential street below. But Katie's interest was piqued, and she crept toward it, her feet breaking the dry, brown plants, her toes curled to protect her soles from pebbles and burrs.

She approached several feet and then paused. The white patch appeared to be a piece of cloth, not nubby like a towel, but a soft, well-washed cotton. It might have been thrown over a bundle of something, or perhaps it was just hooked on various twigs and weeds, so that it stuck up lumpily above ground level. Katie could have stopped, she could have turned back to the path, but she wondered about the cloth, how it had gotten this deep into the trees, and what was under it. She struggled closer, the dry grasses and odd brambles scratching her bare calves, leaving thin, red lines. When she was next to it, she crouched down.

On close inspection, Katie could see that the cloth was a large, loose shirt, probably dropped off the waist of an over-heated biker and blown into the trees. But, it didn't lie in a twist or clump, as a blown object might. It appeared to have been carefully spread, wide and flat. Katie touched the center of the cloth, and she felt something firm beneath it. Unconsciously, she reached up and touched her own injured chin. Then she grabbed the center of the shirt, and she pulled it away.

The face on the ground stared at Katie. It had the palest skin and large, blue eyes, and if Katie had seen it in life she might have thought it beautiful. But it was not alive, it was lying still and cold on the forest floor, its eyes glassy and sightless. A thin trail led from the corner of its lips to the ground, a dried trail of brownish red. Her chest was bare, her arms tucked beneath her so that her small white breasts jutted toward the sky. Someone had tried to dig a trench, but the earth was dry and hard, and he had only managed a low, short trough large enough for her hips and legs. Katie saw them now, hidden beneath a thin hail of dirt and grass and leaves.

Katie felt her own horror push at the skin of her face and arms and legs, a thousand needles jutting from her insides out through her skin. She turned and ran out of the woods and down the path towards home. She completely forgot her skates.

Chapter Fourteen

"Meredith. Any word?"

The three hours since she had last seen him, right here in this same spot, felt like a millennium. She clutched her purse like a life preserver, as Lewis stood anxiously in his kitchen doorway. A faint light glimmered in the backs of his eyes, but her news would extinguish it. At least she hoped so, that the news would deliver the shock of a sharp slap or a punch in the gut. Of course she did not wish him pain. But if he knew already, if she told him and his eyes veiled and his lips pressed into a sly line, that would be much worse.

"Has Laura come home yet?" She thought she knew the answer, but she couldn't be completely sure, not until Lewis erased every shred of hope.

"No. And I don't expect her to. The more I think about it, the more I think her disappearance is part of a plot to steal Marie and torment me."

Lewis was smart, but he was wrong. Maybe he was so tangled up with Laura and his anger toward her that he couldn't see clearly anymore. Or maybe it wasn't just a question of a blind spot. He was the husband, after all. She would be a fool not to suspect him.

He looked at her expectantly. Meredith knew he could see the anticipation in her eyes. She always rushed to the bad, to do it and be done and end the apprehension.

But she hesitated. She had to tell him something terrible, and that hurt her, but she also knew she must force herself away from him, to regain perspective and gage his reaction. She could not jeopardize her own career and this investigation because she had foolishly begun to care for a man who had probably killed his wife.

"Lewis, please sit down." She combed her fingers through her hair and then crossed her arms tightly in front of her. "We have no further information about Marie. But this is very hard. Please, sit," she repeated more gently, indicating a stiff oak chair askew from the kitchen table. Lewis sat, but she remained standing, looking down at him. "This morning, a woman's body was found in Kenilworth near the Greenbay bike trail. She was about thirty-five years old, five-foot eight and thin, with short brown hair. She was wearing a white tee shirt and gray shorts." She would not tell him that the killer had removed the woman's shirt and draped it over her face. Guilty or innocent, this was enough.

Lewis buried his face in his hands. Meredith was silent. She would answer his questions, but she would neither disturb him nor supply extra information. He sat quite still, gripping his face. Meredith wondered what she would see if she pried his fingers away. Finally, he looked up. His cheeks were red, his eyes damp and squinting.

"How did it happen?" he asked.

"I believe her neck was broken. We'll know more this afternoon."

"It might not be Laura," he said.

"You're right.   That's why we need to make sure."

Lewis shivered.   Meredith thought, if he were a child, he would scream and run upstairs and bolt his door.   Instead, he clutched his thighs to try to stop their shaking.

"I'll come with you." she said briskly.   "Let's go now, if you can manage it.   We'll take my car."

Silently, they drove south on Sheridan Road to Evanston Hospital.   Here she had given birth to Maggie and Lucy, and returned later in maternal torment with their broken arms and split chins.   Once she had imagined committing herself here, when the pain of Alexander's betrayal had suffused her, when she knew no man could ever love her, and her life was over. Perhaps Marie had been born here too.   Lewis could imagine Laura and Marie, their ghosts hovering in the antiseptic air.

Clutching the steering wheel, Meredith pulled into the garage and drove methodical circles to a rooftop parking space.   She did not want to do this either, but she must be professional, she must keep herself collected. They walked stoutly to the elevator and exited in the hospital lobby, where unreal people who knew nothing about the dead woman went about their business. An old man gripping a large white plastic bag waited in a wheelchair for his ride home.   A faded mother in a pale smock hoisted a toddler to her hip, next to her pregnant stomach. Doctors and technicians in cotton coats strolled in self-assured clusters. Meredith stopped at the information desk to ask directions and then led Lewis to Elevator C. She pushed the down button. This way to the bowels, she thought. This way to hell.

The basement was cement, a series of gray earthworm tunnels with huge pipes running along the ceiling. An arrow directed visitors to the cafeteria, a vacuous yellow room reeking of grease. Passing hospital personnel toted styrofoam boxes and lidded paper cups. Lewis stopped and leaned against the wall.

"Are you all right? Do you need to sit down?"

"No. I'm okay," he assured her, his face drained. He grabbed her arm, and the contact pierced her. "Sorry," he said.

"Here, Lewis, this is silly," she responded brusquely, her cheeks flushed. "Let's sit down for a minute. It's not going to help anybody if you faint in the hallway." Meredith took his elbow and guided him into the cafeteria, past the nauseating smell of mashed potatoes and cream gravy and salisbury steak, to a gold plastic chair at an empty table. "I'm going to get you a coke. I think it'll make you feel better. Maybe you should put your head down for a minute."

Meredith watched as Lewis obeyed, his gray hair settling against his forearms. He closed his eyes. She swiveled and stepped smack into her ex-husband, Dr. Alexander Bennett.

"Alex! What are you doing here?" she asked stupidly. He was wiry and handsome, comfortingly familiar and distressingly forbidden. His white coat hanging loose over his neat plaid sport shirt, he looked capable and cheering and surprisingly young.

"I work here, remember? I saw you across the cafeteria. What about you?"

"Business. I'm afraid I have to go to the morgue to help with an identification." She shouldn't have done that, admitted a vulnerability. Alexander wasn't her friend, that fact was branded on her soul. He picked up on it immediately.

"I'll bet you're afraid. I remember when Maggie cut her foot and you had to put your head between your knees. You ever done this before?"

Meredith shook her head. She could not let Alexander do this to her. He was being charming and sensitive, the way he was when they first met, the way he wasn't after ten years of marriage, when he had discovered joy with a certain bimbo and dumped her. He had made his choice, she was alone, and she had to manage without him. And yet there was still something still between them. She could feel it in the overheated air, a primal tug. Ten years of sharing trivia and children and an endearingly squeaky bed did not vanish because his crotch had at least temporarily replaced his brain.

"We'll be fine. We just stopped to get a cold drink." She hoped he noticed the "we," and wished absurdly that it would make him suffer.

"Meredith, I've been wanting to thank you. You're doing a great job with the girls. And how are you doing?"

She turned white. He had no right to ask this, to stand there probing her as if he cared about her feelings.

"Yeah, they're great, we're all great. Well, I have to get back to work."

"Okay. It was great to see you." He smiled, then reached across and touched her shoulder. "I know you probably won't believe me, but I think about you a lot, you know." He pressed his lips together, as if he were sealing himself. "Give my love to the girls." Then he turned and walked away.

Meredith watched him go, his strong shoulders, his arms, his smooth, muscled hands gently swinging, and she wanted to rush after him, to hurl herself into those arms and sob the truth, that she missed him, that the last two years had been a terrible mistake. But she couldn't do that, because the mistake wasn't hers. She looked back at Lewis, his head now settled directly against the cool formica. She was not going to distress herself thinking about this, there was nothing to think about. Alexander had made his choice, and she had to live with it. She picked up a paper cup, filled it with ice and coke from the machine, and paid the cashier. When she returned, Lewis was listing a little, but sitting up.

"Here, sip a little of this. They don't seem to have any whiskey down here," She smiled weakly. He stared at the cup and drank a bit. "I'll be all right now," he muttered. "It just hit me for a minute, that's all."

"It'll be over soon," she said. He didn't look at her. They stood and walked carefully down the hall.

Meredith pushed open the heavy steel doors. She was just going to do this and get it done. It couldn't be that bad. So, she would see a dead woman, a woman with a broken neck, who might be Laura Sumner, whom she knew and disliked and had seen alive only yesterday. Meredith wondered what a broken neck looked like, if the head were tilted to one side like a daisy on a snapped stem. An employee with beaded hair looked up from her romance novel.

"I'm Meredith Bennett and this is Lewis Sumner. I believe Dr. Takada is expecting us."

"Please have a seat," the woman said. "I'll tell him you're here."

They sat on molded turquoise fiberglass chairs. Meredith studied Lewis, gazing blankly at the floor. In all probability, he was about to see the body of his wife, a woman he had once loved, and with whom he had created a child. Meredith knew that all their fighting had not eradicated the bond between them, that the fighting was even a part of that bond.

A short, mustached young man in a blue coat and sneakers appeared and smiled incongruously. "This way, please," he said. They followed him through a second set of double doors into a brilliantly lit, sparkling hard room, white light reflecting from the sterile green tiles paving the floor and walls and from two metal tables at its center. The left one was empty, about the shape and size of an adult human corpse, and neatly perforated with rows of small holes for the drainage of fluids. A chopping block perched at its head, and a metal scale dangled eerily over its foot.

The second table supported a sheet-draped mound. Dr. Takada, a tiny, white-haired man in an immaculate buttoned white coat, stood beside it protectively. Meredith nodded to Detective Field, who was already there, and offered her hand to Dr. Takada. Despite her determination to remain aloof, Meredith felt her stomach twist, a primitive recoil from the spectacle of death. Lewis stood frozen near the doors.

"Good afternoon, Dr. Takada. I'm Meredith Bennett, and this is Mr. Sumner."

"Hello. I'm sorry to meet you under such difficult circumstances. Mr. Sumner, I would imagine you are quite anxious right now. It is probably best to do this immediately. Please come here beside me." Dr. Takada opened his arm to summon Lewis and lifted the sheet. It was done almost at once.

"Oh my God," Lewis cried, as everyone stared at Laura's dead face.

Laura's skin was bluish white, her sightless eyes wide and icy, startled into an unnatural stillness. Her hair fell away in a dark tangle. Meredith was relieved to see that she wasn't bloody or hideous, only cold and empty and infinitely sad. The intelligence and intensity that were Laura Sumner had vanished. Laura would never cradle her child or kiss her lover or skewer Lewis again. Surprisingly, Meredith felt the deprivation keenly.

Dr. Takada dropped the sheet and eased Lewis toward the door. "Her neck is broken, and she has some bruising on her head, hip and thigh," he murmured to Meredith. "We'll know more later this afternoon."'

"I'll be back after I take Mr. Sumner home. Come on, Lewis," she said quietly, taking his arm.

He did not resist. She led him, trembling, into the hallway. He turned to her, and he seemed gentle and needy and terribly hurt.

"My God, Meredith, this is so horrible. I never imagined anything could be this horrible."

He said her name, and he wept, and Meredith held him helplessly in her arms. He pressed himself against her, like a child, and like a man, and she tried desperately not to feel it. She had to discover Laura's killer, and she had to find Marie. That was her job, and it mattered more than anything else, more than her petty career concerns and her children's goodnight kisses and her own loneliness and fear and jealousy. She owed it to Laura, and she owed it to herself. And she had to start with Lewis Sumner, now pressed warm against her breast.

In the car, back on Sheridan Road, she questioned him.

"You told me that you and Laura had a fight last night, and she ran out. What time was that?"

"About ten o'clock."

"What did you fight about?"

"Her affair with Richard Orwell. I told her that I knew about it, and I was afraid he had taken Marie. She was shocked that I knew, and that I didn't seem to care, and I think her pride was hurt. I had never bothered to confront her about it before. Our marriage was over. It didn't seem to matter."

"So, she left. Did she say where she was going?"

"No, she just ran out. She didn't take her purse. I doubt she had any money. She was pretty upset." He wiped his nose.

Meredith turned left onto Cherry. "What did you do after that?"

"I went to bed. I figured she was a big girl, she was probably just taking a walk to cool off, or maybe she would call her boyfriend. I wasn't worried about her, just about Marie. I decided I'd talk to you about Orwell in the morning, and I did."

"Did you have any contact with Laura after ten o'clock last night?"

"No. I wish to God I had. Maybe I could have prevented this somehow. You know Laura and I didn't get along, but I never wanted this."

Meredith stopped her car in front of the Sumners' house, now Lewis's alone. "I'm going to let you off here. Don't leave town."

"You've got to believe me, Meredith. You of all people." She looked at him steadily. "I'll talk to you later." He closed the car door and shuffled, head down, toward the empty house.

Meredith sat still in the car for a moment. She wanted to believe Lewis, but his word wasn't enough anymore. She needed to find an independent witness who had seen Laura leave the house under her own power last night, to corroborate his story. But Winnetka was so quiet, hardly even a squirrel on the street at ten o'clock on a weeknight. She would have the police check with the neighbors. Maybe someone was out strolling the golden retriever.

She stepped on the gas and drove past the Ramseys' house, the scene of so much salivating yesterday with the news of Mike's unsavory past. Parked patrol cars and evidence vans meant that the police were still searching, and a few rubbernecks chatted idly on the front sidewalk. Of course, Meredith thought. The T.V. news.

Channel Six aired live reports from the scene of the latest Chicagoland atrocities on its ten o'clock broadcast. In all likelihood, a news team had stationed itself outside the Ramseys' house last night to cover the story of Mike's history and his connection to Marie's disappearance. If Laura had left the house last night around ten, as Lewis had said, she might have walked past the T.V. crew on her way to town.

Meredith stopped at a pay phone and called Channel Six. A news team had indeed broadcast from the Ramseys' last night, and several neighbors had emerged to enjoy the excitement. One neighbor had noticed Laura Sumner hurrying past on the other side of the street, and the reporter had practically tackled her, but she had rushed away. The crew had remained in front of the Ramseys' until around eleven, and they had not seen Laura return. Hallelujah, praise the Lord, Lewis had told the truth.

If she could track Laura's movements, Meredith thought, she would surely find the killer. The question, then, was where Laura had gone. Meredith tried to imagine herself in Laura's place, distraught and penniless, out on the street. She wouldn't hitchhike, that was too dangerous. The stores were closed, and she had no money for a movie or a drink or a hotel. Undoubtedly, she would try to get to a phone to call her lover for help. But according to his secretary, Richard Orwell was in New York last night. Meredith would have to double-check that.

Laura certainly wouldn't have called her mother-in-law, they despised each other, and she wasn't chummy with the neighbors. She was far too busy to have cultivated friends. Which, without Richard Orwell, left her quite alone, walking in circles late at night in the same neighborhood as Mike Ramsey. Mike was local, he was a criminal, and he was a suspect in Marie's kidnapping. And two terrible crimes could not occur in the same Winnetka family within days of each other without being somehow connected.

Mike was a child molester, and Laura Sumner was not a child. But her shirt had been removed, a suggestion of sexual assault, and she had not been raped. Mike Ramsey did not rape either, he just liked to touch, and obviously, Laura would not have wanted him to touch her. Unlike a child, she would have fought back. Dr. Takada had said that Laura had bruises on her head, hip, and thigh. If Mike had attacked her and she had struggled, she might have fallen from some height and broken her neck.

Laura's body had been discovered near the train station, where enormous flights of stairs travelled down from street level to the platform and tracks. Laura might have planned to use the telephone or take a train, perhaps to some acquaintance downtown or Richard or even to the office. She probably knew the conductors, maybe they would give her a free ride. Mike might have noticed her through the window when she passed his house and then followed, slipping out the back to avoid the news team.

The Winnetka beach was another possibility, another local spot with a treacherous flight of stairs. The beach would be a logical place to walk alone and think. If Mike had followed Laura and killed her there, he would have had to haul her body up all those stairs and across the park to a car, to transport her the eight blocks to the bike path. But Mike was young and strong and desperate. The task would be strenuous, but probably not impossible.

Meredith called Joe Field. He said that the police had finished processing the crime scene and had observed faint marks, like rollerblade tracks, in the hard dirt off the bike path near Laura's body. The weeds in the area were also noticeably trampled, but they did not yield the hoped-for stray button or blood drop. At Meredith's urging, he promised to send officers to check the beach and the train station.

Hurriedly, Meredith drove back to the Ramsey's alley, parked, and walked to the back door. Through its gauze-curtained window, she could see Mike planted at the kitchen table, his head bowed over a magazine. His mother, in a dress and apron, wandered past with a dust mop. Meredith rang the bell, and Mike jumped.

Chapter Fifteen

Mike wanted to run, he wanted to hide upstairs under the bed, but he couldn't. She had already seen him. He couldn't even sit in his own kitchen without the police peeking at him through the curtains. He sounded crazy, he thought, as if he believed aliens were watching him through the electric outlets, but the problem was, his whole life had gone crazy. The D.A. was at the back door, the police were turning his house upside down, his neighbors were on the front lawn swinging the noose, and his mother spent her afternoons simmering pots of poison soup. It didn't matter how hard he tried. He would never be free, never.

He opened the door and sat back down at the table. She might as well show herself in, the house was practically public property. His mother came in from the dining room.

"Why, Ms. Bennett, hello." How nice to see you, Mike thought, automatically, but his mother wouldn't say that. She didn't lie about the little things. "Let me just turn down the stove, and we'll go into the living room."

The soup gurgled, filling the room with acrid steam. His mother didn't eat much in warm weather, but she insisted that Mike consume a big bowl every night. A grown man like Mike had to keep up his strength, she said. But he was getting weaker and more lethargic, and he had trouble focusing, and then he couldn't sleep.

He knew he wasn't a comfort to his mother anymore, he was a humiliation, just as his father had been. And he knew that she was a tidy person who liked to clear away her messes promptly and with a minimum of fuss. He wondered how much longer he would be able to walk, and if anyone would put up a ramp for him. Well, he guessed he wouldn't need one. The only way he was leaving this house was in handcuffs or a box. Only jail could save his life. But he had heard stories about jail, terrifying ones, especially about what inmates do to child molesters. He couldn't go to jail. He would rather be dead.

"Thank you, Mrs. Ramsey, but I really need to talk to Mike. Alone, if you don't mind."

"I hate to be rude, but I think he ought to have his lawyer here before you start asking him a lot of questions."

"It's all right, Mom." Mike closed his magazine. He couldn't stand the lawyer his mother had hired, with his greasy hair and baggy suit and a mouth that looked like it was tasting something bad. His mother frowned, but she left. He could feel her dusting the dining room, right next door.

Ms. Bennett sat down next to him. "Mike, where were you last night, starting from about six o'clock?"

"I was home. I haven't left the house for days." He ruffled the magazine pages and stared at them blankly. The magazine appeared to lift from the table, and soon he saw two of them, just drifting.

"So, what did you do during the evening?"

He bit his lip. "We ate dinner and we watched T.V. I took a shower, and I went to bed."

"That's you and your mother."

"Yeah."

"What time did you go to bed?"

"It was around eleven. There were some reporters in front last night, and it was noisy until they left." He tried hard to align his eyes, and the magazines consolidated and fell to the table. "What's going on?"

"I'm afraid that Laura Sumner was found dead this morning. She may have been murdered."

The blood drained from Mike's face, and he started to shake. His mother ran into the room. "You're not going to pin that on him, too!" she shrieked. "We've lived here for years. We go to church. I have a reputation! Mike was home with me all night last night, all of it. I'm sorry for that woman, but this is an outrage. It's a witch hunt, that's what it is. If you have anything further to ask my son, you call his lawyer."

Ms. Bennett stood. "I'm terribly sorry to bring you such bad news. I just want to talk to the officers here for a moment. Then I'll go. I'll be in touch." Calmly, she left the room.

Mike's mother touched her hair and smoothed her dress. He could see she was trying to settle herself down. "This whole thing is ridiculous, just ridiculous. I hope you don't take it too much to heart, Mike. Soon they'll find the real culprit, and this nightmare will end. Well, it's almost dinnertime, though I couldn't eat a bite with all this commotion. Help me set the table, please."

He breathed deeply, inhaling the soup's toxic perfume. It was hard for him to get up, hard to stand. His mother's secret recipe was working again. If he was going to do anything, he would have to do it soon.

Meredith climbed into the driver's seat. Mike was with his mother who loved him, the same alibi he had for the night Marie was kidnapped. But what he had said didn't matter as much as what she had seen. She remembered his clean brown face and his naked arms pricked with curling hairs, and his strong, tanned hands. He was clean and golden and unmarked, no bruises, no scratches, no redness or broken skin. Laura Sumner would never have allowed Mike, a virtual stranger and a suspect in the kidnapping of her daughter, to get hold of her in the night, alone in the dark, not without an enormous struggle. Laura would have scratched and kicked and slapped and bitten, anything she could do to repel him. But, as far as Meredith could see, she had not laid a hand on him.

Back in her own office cubicle, Meredith fingered the pink slip of paper. Richard Orwell had deigned to return her call, and he had left his Chicago office number. Apparently, he had returned early from his business trip to New York. Now, the question was, how early? If he had just arrived this afternoon, or even this morning, he had an alibi for Laura's murder. But if he came home last night, concealed his presence from his secretary, and then stayed away from the office this morning, that was suspicious. Meredith picked up her desk phone and punched in his number.

"Mr. Orwell's office."

"Yes, is he in, please? This is Ms. Bennett, returning his call."

"I'm sorry, he's in a meeting. May I have him call you?"

"We've been trading messages for some time now, and I'm afraid it's rather important. I would very much appreciate it if you would find him for me. I'll hold."

"I'm sorry. Mr. Orwell is in an important meeting, and he left specific instructions that I was not to disturb him. I will be happy to tell him that you called."

"Thank you."

Meredith hung up. The important meeting might well relate to Laura's death, which by now would be public knowledge. She dialed her next door neighbor, who graciously agreed to pick up the kids at camp. Then she punched in her own home phone number. "Hi, Maggie, it's Mom. I have to work late tonight. I'm sorry, but you know it hardly ever happens. Why don't you guys just stick some hot dogs in the microwave, and you can take out some chips. And peel a couple carrots. I'm not sure when I'll be home, but I'll try not to be too late. I love you. Don't use the stove. There's ice cream in the freezer, or you can walk to Baskin Robbins. I'll pay you back. Don't lock yourselves out. Bye, Honey, bye, Luce."

Meredith returned to the parking garage and retrieved her car. She was a terrible mother, leaving her ten-year-old to fix her eight-year-old a revolting dinner and watch premarital sex on T.V. But tonight she had to talk to Richard Orwell regarding the murder of Laura Sumner. She was not going to relinquish this case to someone else.

She rolled down the windows as she pressed down Lake Shore Drive past joggers and sailboats, grass against lake against sky. Soon she penetrated the city, drove into a parking garage near Richard Orwell's office, and ascended the levels of darkness. She parked, glanced around her, and stepped out of the car.

Meredith did not like Chicago parking garages. They were dim and isolated and women got raped in them, sometimes even murdered. Heels echoing, she crossed the cement to the elevator. She pushed the down button and heard a slow, responsive whir. That was good. In two minutes she would be back on the street.

The door opened. A man stood in the elevator, a well-dressed man, patiently waiting for Meredith to enter. She glanced at him casually, pretending she wasn't anxious, that she routinely enclosed herself in four-foot square steel cubicles with strange men in downtown Chicago. She entered and, in a gesture of trust, turned her back to him. The door closed.

Slowly, the elevator gears ground, and she felt herself motion. They were going down. In a minute, less than that, they would be at street level, and the doors would open again. But the man still had time, he had plenty of time. All he had to do was reach up, push the red button, and stop the elevator. He wouldn't do that, he was wearing a suit, he was probably a lawyer with a pretty wife and a townhouse in Lincoln Park. But he was a man, and she was a woman. Ultimately, that was all that mattered. He had the ability to hurt her, and she was afraid.

The door opened. Meredith glanced up at the lighted panel. They were on the ground floor. The man stepped forward and placed his hand next to Meredith, holding the door for her. "Thank you," she murmured. She emerged, blinking, into the haze.

Meredith hurried down the block to the First National Bank building, its wide base flared like a cement skirt. She discovered the proper elevator bank and ascended alone. On the fiftieth floor the doors opened, the title "Winters & Early" rising from the marble walls like the word of the Lord. Meredith slipped down the hall, turned the corner, and discovered a door labeled "Richard Orwell." His secretary, a large blonde with sharp red fingernails, glanced up.

"Hello. I'm Meredith Bennett. We spoke on the phone." Meredith smiled pleasantly and read the name plate. "And you must be Linda Purvis. I'm a prosecutor investigating Laura Sumner's death." Linda's eyes gleamed. "As I'm sure you understand, I need to interview her friends and associates as quickly as possible. I would be very grateful if you would help me get in touch with Mr. Orwell. Also, I was wondering when he returned from New York."

Linda squinted. "I'm really not sure. He came into the office early this afternoon, around one o'clock, I'd say. But he made his own return reservation when his plans changed."

"Thank you. That's very helpful."

Meredith waited. Linda hesitated, then stood up. "It's a terrible thing," she said, "first the baby, and now this. I certainly want to help in any way I can. I'll go get Mr. Orwell from his meeting."

Richard walked carefully down the gray-carpeted hall. He knew that he must appear calm, and he tightened his shoulders and clenched his arms. Turning the corner, his right knee gave beneath him, but he caught himself, not by flailing and toward some stable external object, but through his own force of will. Now he could see the prosecutor hovering outside his office. She wore a limp cotton dress, and her hair frizzed around her face like a storm cloud. She was no Laura, he thought, but there would never be another Laura, and he couldn't think about that now. Drab and crumpled though she was, Ms. Bennett represented the power of the state. A lack of style did not diminish her dangerousness.

"Please, come in." He summoned her into his office and shut the door. "I understand from my secretary that you've come regarding Laura Sumner." His black leather chair cradled him, as his hands clung together on the desk.

"I'm Meredith Bennett, state's attorney. Nice to meet you, Mr. Orwell. I'm sorry about Ms. Sumner. I understand that the two of you were quite close."

"Two doors down, as you see."

"Yes." Ms. Bennett paused. "I called you yesterday, and your secretary said you had gone to New York for a few days. I'm glad you managed to come back early."

Richard smiled. "I live in the ever-shifting world of the client's convenience and the adversary's delay. I'm sure you understand."

"And when did you arrive back in Chicago?"

Richard considered. "Yesterday evening."

"On what flight?" "I believe it was the six o'clock out of LaGuardia."

"So, you landed in Chicago at about seven-thirty and arrived home around eight-fifteen?"

"Yes, that sounds about right. Where exactly is this headed, Meredith?" He hoped he sounded charming and familiar, perhaps paternal.

"Did you see Ms. Sumner last night?"

Richard inhaled sharply and pushed his chair back. "Meredith, I am shocked and saddened by Laura's death. I'm not sure what you're implying with these questions, but if you mean to suggest that I might have had anything to do with it, then you will have to excuse me. I am happy to cooperate, but I believe at this point I am entitled to advice of counsel."

"You are not under arrest, Mr. Orwell. I am simply trying to establish a few basic facts. Frankly, I'm astonished that you find these mundane questions so threatening, and I'm sorry you don't feel more of a responsibility to bring your partner's murderer to justice. I suggest you locate a lawyer for yourself, and that you make yourselves available for a conversation in my office at the North Suburban Courthouse in Skokie tomorrow morning at nine o'clock.   Until then." Meredith stood and walked out the door.

Richard sank back into his chair. He rested his head in his hands, and the sensation of his own flesh against his fingers, the realization that this was the feel of his own body, that he was a limited physical being and not the powerful spirit he usually imagined himself to be, jarred and frightened him. This is my nose, he thought, it has a bone inside, this is my skin, rough and whiskery and aging, this is my face, just like anyone else's face, just like Laura's face, which has ceased to live, and which will soon begin to decay, until it is just bone, and then soon, soon beyond belief, it will be nothing at all. It is already nothing at all.

He shook his head to eliminate the blackness and pushed the intercom button on his phone. "Linda, thanks for staying. Let's call it a day," he said mechanically. He had to get out of here.

Meredith exited the elevator in the bank lobby, found a pay phone, and called her voice mail, which retrieved an excited message from Joe Field. "Meredith, we talked to Richard Orwell's neighbors this afternoon. Well, we didn't have much hope. Who notices anything in the city? But his next-door neighbor says that at around eleven o'clock last night he was getting ready to go to bed, locking up the windows, and he glanced outside and saw a cab stopped in front. He wouldn't have thought much of it, but it was a turquoise cab, and he thought it was kind of strange. He watched for a minute and a tall, dark haired woman came out of Richard Orwell's house. It looked like she paid the cabdriver. The cab left, and she went back into Orwell's place. Well, I called Three-O-Three Cabs, and one of their guys took a woman from the Winnetka train station to the Gold Coast last night at around ten-fifteen. We checked with the airlines, and low and behold, Richard Orwell came home last night on a six o'clock flight, plenty of time for him to have a nice visit with Laura Sumner at eleven. So maybe Orwell did it. But I don't know how she ended up back in Winnetka on the bike path."

Meredith called Joe back. "I just saw Orwell, and he didn't admit to his relationship .with Laura or to seeing her last night. First thing in the morning, we've got to get a warrant to search his house and car. Anything turn up at the Ramseys'?"

"Not there. But listen to this. We went to the beach and the train station, like you said, to check out the stairs. I really didn't have much hope. I mean, she breaks her neck, so we check the big stairways -- what are the odds, if you'll pardon me? Well, I suppose we both turned out to be right, in a way. The train station turned up zip, a few old newspapers and cardboard cups, nothing we could connect to Laura Sumner. Then the guys went to the beach. We didn't find anything obvious there either, and with all the sand and half the North Shore wandering through, it's pretty hard ·to come up with stray hairs. But they were down in the sand, digging a little around the stairs, looking for blood or a button or something, you know, on the off chance. At first they just found some cigarette butts and gum wrappers and a couple of plastic shovels that had probably been there for twenty years. And then Ed, he calls out that he hit something, and he pulls up this black plastic bag. You'd figure it might be beer cans or something some kids didn't clean up, but Ed said that for some reason they both got real quiet. It was like they sensed this could be it, and they were, you know, awestruck. Well, Dave grabbed hold of the bag, and Ed ripped it open. And you know what it was? You'll never believe it. Tapes! This bag was stuffed with cassette tapes. They didn't know what the hell they were, but they took them back to the station and started listening to them, and then they called me. You won't believe it, Meredith. They're Mike Ramsey's tapes. He says, "This is Mike Ramsey," and the date, just as stupid as could be. He taped all his wildest fantasies about the Winnetka preschool set, believe me, it's sickening, he's a real pervert. And guess who he wanted to do it with? Marie Sumner."

*

Meredith turned the key in her lock and pushed open the front door. Although the house was dark, it was only 9:30, and she braced herself for the tumbled assault or at least the groggy shuffle of her two young daughters. But the house was quiet. She closed the door behind her and walked the few steps to Lucy's bedroom. The bed was neatly made, Lucy's stuffed kitten collection lined up symmetrically against the pillow. She crossed the hall. Except for two comic books and a candy bar wrapper, Maggie's bed was also undisturbed. She checked her own room. Empty. Her children were gone. Her stomach flipped, and she felt a low level of panic. She had forgotten her priorities, and here she was involved in a kidnapping case, and she had gotten too close to some sinister underground mob, and they had taken Maggie and Lucy off to some rat-infested tenement as revenge. But that was preposterous, this was not some Bruce Willis movie, this was the North Shore, or close enough. Quickly, she tapped down the hall and punched the message button next to the flashing red light on her answering machine.

"Hi, Mom, it's Maggie. We're at Dad's. Shawna called to ask about this weekend, and when I told her you weren't here, she invited us to the beach cause Dad was working late too, and then afterwards she brought us over here to play with this new Sega she bought us. It's really cool. Since you're still not home, we're just going to sleep over here. She says she'll take us to camp in the morning, and if you have to work late any more, you should just let her know, cause she'd be glad to have us if she doesn't have plans with Dad or something. Bye.

Bye. Meredith pushed the rewind button. So, the girls were safe, of course, and happy to boot. It was really very nice of the lovely Shawna to take them under her wing like that. She licked her lips, hesitated, and then picked up the phone and punched in the number she used to share with Alexander.

"Hola!"

"Hello, Shawna? It's Meredith. You have the girls?"

"Yep. I hope it's alright. I know I probably should've asked first, but they sounded kind of bummed out, and they had a blast at the beach. They're kind of asleep now. You want to talk to them?"

"No, that's not necessary. I just wanted to tell you that I'm home, if they need me for anything."

"Oh, no, they're fine. We had a great swim, and we found loads of sea glass for their collection. I had them take a shower, so don't worry about that, and they zeed right out. I'll take them to camp tomorrow, cause it's sort of on my way to my doctor's appointment anyway."

Meredith paused. She wouldn't ask. It wasn't any of her business, and it would be ungracious under the circumstances to hope she had contracted a terminal disease. "Thank you very much. As I'm sure you realize, I'm almost invariably at home at night, but I'm working on a big case right now, and I needed to give it some extra attention. So, it was lucky you hit the one day I was late, and thanks for helping out."

"No problem. I really loved it. You know, in a way, they're my kids too, at least, that's the way I feel. I'd be glad to have them anytime, I mean, if Al and I don't have any previous engagements."

"Mmmhmm. Well. In the morning, they'll need sack lunches. They like peanut butter. And they'll need their swimsuits and towels."

"Okay, no problem. Oh, here he comes, finally. Bye."

Bye. Meredith hung up the phone, imagining Shawna rushing toward Al in slow motion, the slurp of wet kisses, and the skid of khaki against lycra. Shawna had stolen Meredith's husband, and now she was working on her children.

Well, tough. No matter how many Nordstrom's bags and cupcakes she gave them, Shawna would never be their mother. She was their stepmother, and everyone, especially Maggie and Lucy, who adored Grimms' fairytales, knew that stepmothers were evil and jealous, unlike real mothers, who could turn into shrubs and give you a hand even when they were dead. Ultimately, after some period of seduction, Maggie and Lucy would realize this, and so would Shawna. And Alexander. And they wouldn't sue for custody because she had worked late on an interesting case for once in a blue moon and finish ruining her life.

Realizing she was starving, she slipped off her shoes and tromped into the kitchen. She would spread herself a crummy sandwich as fast as she could and then unwind in front of the T.V. news. Nothing like a few drive-by shootings to relax you after a hard day chasing murderers and having your children bewitched by their stepmother. Then she would catch a few of those zees herself. Between Mike Ramsey and Richard Orwell, tomorrow promised to be another hectic day.

Chapter Sixteen

Angelica had left the hospital Wednesday afternoon, and she stayed home all day Thursday, sweating in front of a cheap dime store fan puffing heat at the shredded couch. She had no job anymore. The Sumners had no use for her without Marie. Lewis seemed to have no thought for her at all, that when she had no work, she had no money. She supposed she had expected him to keep paying her in case Marie turned up again, or at least to give her a few weeks' salary, to tide her over. Soon the rent would be due, and she didn't have it.

She wasn't having second thoughts, not exactly. But she hadn't quite thought things through. She had wanted a baby, and her only child, the child she had comforted and fed and bathed and loved five days a week practically since the day she was born, Marie, could have been ripped from her at any moment. The Sumners were divorcing, they might move, they didn't know, they didn't care. They had no respect for Angelica and the love she had created. And Laura was no kind of mother, working all the time. But now Angelica realized that, Marie or no Marie, she had to work too. Somebody had to provide food and clothes and pay the rent. But how could she work when she couldn't even leave the house? She couldn't ask her sister Anita for help everyday as she had on Tuesday and Wednesday, Anita had her own troubles, and she wasn't that stupid. Soon she would figure it out.

Angelica turned on the television. She flipped around, past the baseball games and the hospital shows. When she reached the ten o'clock news, she froze. Staring out from the screen, her likeness bashed into a zillion fragments and then reconstructed in Angelica's living room, was Laura Sumner. "I trusted you in my house," her eyes blazed, "with my baby and my husband, with everything that was precious to me. I gave you Marie everyday, but that wasn't enough for you. How could you hurt me this way? I was trying to do my best for Marie. Do you really think you can do any better?"

From behind Laura's glare, Angelica heard the newscaster's drone become louder and more animated until she could discern the words. "Ms. Sumner's body was found in a wooded area of Winnetka along the Greenbay bicycle trail. Police will not say whether they believe her death is connected to the disappearance earlier this week of her daughter Marie. They confirm that they have a number of leads, and they expect to make an arrest shortly."

Laura couldn't be dead. This was absurd. How could two such things happen in a single family in a single week and not be related? But Angelica hadn't killed her. She had disliked Laura, she had been jealous of her, but she had never wished her any serious harm. But what if Laura had been searching for Marie? Maybe she had been looking along the bike path, alone in the dark, tearing the weeds, groping along the ground, trying to find her baby. And then someone, some horrible man who hates women, had crept up and tortured her and murdered her. Maybe Angelica had started the chain of events that led haphazardly but surely to her death.

She turned off the T.V. and shuffled into the bedroom, hardly a room at all, just big enough for a twin bed and a box of clothes. She gazed at the huddled golden child, sleeping sweetly, her curls pasted wet to her scalp. All she wanted to do was live a quiet life and love her baby. But things had become so complicated. She could hardly tell what was right and wrong anymore, and she didn't know how to proceed. Lewis was probably miserable right now, and she had liked Lewis, they had gotten along fine, and a lot of his suffering was her fault. And she needed a job, she needed money, she couldn't care for herself and a child without food, without an apartment. She must talk to someone, someone she could trust. She thought of the church, the cool darkness, the certainty of right and wrong, the comforting peace. Maybe she could talk to a priest. He would know what was right, and he would keep her secret. He would help her figure out what to do next.

*

"Switch that thing off. I'm going to bed."

Carolyn Ramsey turned her face from the television news and walked toward the stairs. Mike knew she couldn't stand the Sumners' ugliness in her living room, among her polished end tables and scrubbed white walls. She looked older, not with the knowledge that her son might be a murderer, a legacy, after all, passed through the maternal line, but with the fear that now her neighbors would condemn her. She would have to figure out how to save herself. If she could come out the victim, a pitiful woman inflicted with a twisted son, then she would be all right. But she wouldn't want to admit it, about the son. A woman's son was her accomplishment, her pride. It would be far better if the son were to die early, in the relative grace of the neighbors' uncertainty, than to continue in life convicted of a heartless crime.

Mike knew she would have to kill him soon. The police had a suspect. They must have found the tapes. Not that they needed the tapes to convict him once they had decided he was a hopeless creep, but that certainly iced the cake. The police would probably be around tomorrow, or that Bennett woman, to arrest him in full view of the neighbors and television cameras.

His mother would have to poison his morning orange juice if she wanted to be sure to beat the police. But soup was her style. Conveniently, there was a small pot left over from dinner, perfect for his lunch. Mike could still taste the metal from his suppertime portion, and he knew she was increasing the dose. He was tired and weak, and he felt sick all the time, but it was still not enough to kill him. If the police would only wait until tomorrow afternoon, she could put a heaping helping in his lunchtime soup and watch him die while she washed the pot. After she had scrubbed away all the evidence, she would call an ambulance, just as she had with Mike's father. The distress of being investigated must have been too much for his heart, she would say. He had always been sickly, just like his father.

In a way, his mother was right. Because if the police were coming tomorrow to slam him in jail for two murders, he would rather die. He had tried so hard to stay on the right path, but once you've left the straight line, they'll hound you forever. He was a fool to think that anyone would believe him, that he could live quietly in the suburbs with his mother. Now that people knew what he had done with that girl years ago, they would assume that he, like some demon, was responsible for every evil thing that happened.

But it wasn't fair, it wasn't fair that he should pay the price for someone else's crimes. And there was only one person to blame for his mistakes, and that was the woman who had prevented him from developing like normal boys and who had killed his father along the way. Mike was not going to let his mother get off scot-free, to receive casseroles and polish the dining room table and sit rigidly in church until the end of time. She had poisoned his father, and she had as good as murdered Mike years ago. She was a smothering, controlling witch, and she would have to pay. He would finally behave like a man, not a puppet. There was no point in his living, she was right about that. But this time, he would remove her mask.

Mike went into the kitchen and opened the cupboard below the sink. Her cleaning solutions, like toy soldiers, stood neatly in the wire basket attached to the inside of the cupboard door. He pulled them out and examined their warning labels. Most simply advised drinking a glass of water if accidentally ingested. He needed something more certainly deadly. The furniture oil read, "harmful or fatal if swallowed." He didn't like the option, but quite a lot of it would probably do the trick. When he shook the can, the fluid sloshed thickly, and the dregs around the cap smelled nasty, and with his stomach queasy already, he wasn't sure he could accomplish it.

Mike wished he knew what his mother used in the soup. It was reasonably palatable, and it had obviously done the job on his father. He searched the cupboards and the refrigerator, but he couldn't find any rat poison or prescription bottles. Well, he did enjoy the irony of ruining his mother with her own cleaning fluid. Certainly all he had become was a nasty stain in her life.

The furniture oil had a plastic safety cap instructing, "Twist and Flip," but at first he couldn't do it. He got a knife out of the kitchen drawer and dug until finally, the top popped off. Damn! He was supposed to shake the stuff too. He pushed the cap back on, shook for a minute, and then repeated the process with the knife. He removed the leftover soup from the refrigerator and poured in a small amount of the oil. It was horrible stuff. Even a little bit created an awful reek and a slimy consistency, and he didn't know what heating it up would do. Well, too bad and too late, because he would be dead and the poison would be in the soup in the refrigerator, and the police would put two and two together, and that would be that.

As an afterthought, he took a dishtowel and wiped the pot and the oil can, to remove his fingerprints.

148

Then he put the pot back in the refrigerator, wrapped the can in the dishtowel, and prepared to drink. He just had to hold his nose and choke it down. It would only take a moment, a slight effort of will. Lord knew he had will power, the tapes would attest to that, if only the police would look beyond the superficial and see what they were really about, how hard he was trying. But the police never looked beyond the surface of anything.

Mike put the can down. He realized that, if he wanted to be certain that his mother was accused of his murder, he must make things very clear and easy for the police. Otherwise, they might never look in the soup pot at all. They would see the nice little old lady and the dead pervert son, and they would figure the son had offed himself, and about time too, the thoughtless bastard, doing it right under his mommy's nose and on her nice clean floor. This would be tricky, because he had to leave a clue so obvious that even the police would find it and understand it, but not so plain that his mother would discover it first. He could leave a note, but she might look for that, and it was hardly his style anyway. Tapes were his style. He would leave one final tape, the voice of vengeance from beyond the grave.

Mike went upstairs and gathered his tape recorder and a blank tape from his dresser. He brought them into the bathroom. If she heard him, his mother would think he was just taking a shower before bed. He took off his clothes, turned the water on, pushed the record button, and stepped under the spray.

"This is Michael Ramsey. Today is July 18. If you find this after I am dead, I want you to know that my mother poisoned me. She also poisoned my father. She shouldn't get away with it. It's not fair, and who knows where she might strike next. I did not take Marie Sumner or kill Laura Sumner, but she and I both know that no one will believe me. Just check the soup pot in the refrigerator. That's all."

Mike turned off the water. Carefully, he dried himself and put on his bathrobe and clean underpants. He left his damp towel and dirty clothes in a heap on the bathroom floor. His mother wouldn't be able to reprimand him about slovenliness this time, he thought grimly. He took the tape recorder back to his room and left it on the dresser. The police knew he made tapes. They just might look.

Mike returned downstairs. The furniture oil sat on the kitchen table, the top gaping open, just as he had left it. He sat in the kitchen chair and lifted the can with the dishtowel. Grimacing, he plugged his nose, pressed his lips around the plastic mouth, and tipped the can back. The thick, greasy liquid oozed down his throat, and he choked. It burned a little, and the taste in his mouth was vile, far worse than anything he had ever tasted before. He paused, and for a moment he wondered whether his mother was really poisoning him after all. But the soup tasted of metal, he knew there was a poison like that, and look what had happened to his father. He tipped the can back again for another large swig. Then he rinsed his mouth with water straight from the tap. Already, he felt dizzy, his stomach knotted, and he was beginning to sweat. He returned the can to its spot on the cupboard door, set the dish towel on the counter, and struggled into the living room. Lifting his knees to his chest, he lay down on the best couch to die.

*

Upstairs, Carolyn Ramsey could not sleep. She didn't dare open her bedroom windows at night with all these kidnappers and murderers on the loose, and she was stifling. Perhaps a shower would help, though it was so late and her hair would look dreadful tomorrow if she slept on it wet. Well, she ought to have time to fix it properly in the morning. She wasn't expecting any callers, and her so-called neighbors would have to take her as she was.

The television had said that the police would make an arrest soon. Carolyn was certain that Mike had been home all last night, and it only made sense that the same person was responsible for both Sumner crimes. It must be the husband. You never could tell about people, and the neighbors were certainly the last to know. Carolyn never would have predicted that he would annihilate his whole family. His wife, maybe, but never his child. Only a monster would murder his own child.

Her warm feet tapping the cool wooden floor, Carolyn tiptoed to the bathroom. Mike had certainly left a mess. She thought she had drummed that out of him, but every so often he would rebel. Well, if he wanted to live in this house, he would have to abide by her rules. Perhaps he really oughtn't to be living with her anymore, she thought, he was practically a grown man. She probably could afford to give him a little rent money, to get him started. It might be better, especially after all this publicity. He really wasn't wanted in Winnetka. She had been trying to protect him, to keep an eye on him after his troubles. But if he had a chance to live on his own in a new community, he might be able to blend in, he might just be able to live a normal life. She had enjoyed taking care of him, before this Sumner business, but now that everything was out in the open, it might be better for both of them if he left.

Stepping under the water, she realized that, for the first time in decades, she wouldn't have to pick up Mike's dirty clothes, wash his dishes, and make his meals anymore. She could use the rest, after all these years. She had to admit, her own standards had dropped with this trouble lately. She hadn't even made her own soup this week, just opened a can of Progresso and dropped in a few extra carrots. She had thought it tasted a bit tinny, but Mike hadn't complained, and she didn't think he'd noticed. Just went to show how much he appreciated her efforts over the years. He had been looking a little unwell lately. It was probably his nerves. This whole business was enough to affect anyone's stomach.

Carolyn soaped her body, and the big, fluffy bubbles, the slick soap and the cool water, gave her genuine pleasure. Perhaps Mike would be happier living away from her, she thought, and she would have less work to do, and she could spend more time taking care of herself. She deserved it. She stepped out and dried herself gently with a clean towel and dropped her light nightgown back over her head. She stepped from the bathroom, and the warm air felt cooler against her damp skin.

Pointedly, Carolyn poked into Mike's room and dropped his dirty clothes and towel on his bedroom floor. Perhaps this would be the last time. Despite her aggravation with his slovenliness, she felt a wave of tenderness and regret. She looked toward the dark bed, to admire his soft face and his strong, young form. But the bed was still made. Mike was gone. He had showered and changed and left.

Carolyn clasped her hands together, and then she hugged herself. Her eyes welled, and she felt for a moment that she might scream, but she kept it inside. "I do not see this," she decided. "Mike is asleep in bed, as usual, and I am dreaming. I never shower at night, that would muss my hair terribly. This is all just a dream." Carefully, she walked back to her room. She closed the door, climbed into bed, and forced her eyes shut.

Chapter Seventeen

At seven o'clock on Friday morning, Meredith stood outside Richard Orwell's townhouse with Detective Joe Field, a gaggle of his police assistants, and a search warrant. She rang the doorbell and gazed up at the living room window's thick curved glass.

"Do you think he's here?" Detective Field peered at the empty window.

"He has an appointment with me at the courthouse at nine. He ought to be shaving or something. Maybe he's in the shower. Let's give him a couple more rings. I'd rather avoid any dramatic huffing and puffing, if it's all the same to you. No matter what happens, this guy is going to hire himself a team of very persnickety lawyers, and I don't want his new front door coming out of my paycheck." Meredith rang the bell again. They all waited.

Finally, Richard appeared, in a navy blue bathrobe decorated with duck decoys. His graying hair stuck up like a kitten's, and dark sockets cradled his eyes. He looked blurrily handsome, as if filmed through a gelled lense. This was the after-hours Richard, thought Meredith, the man that Laura had known. He waited in the open doorway, his naked, furred legs protruding vulnerably from the bottom of his robe.

"Mr. Orwell, we know that Laura was here Wednesday night at about eleven. According to the pathologist, she died between midnight and four a.m. You have been secretive and obstructive. We're coming in. We have a search warrant."

"May I see it?"

Meredith handed him the paper.

"I thought we had a nine o'clock appointment this morning," he said, scanning it.

"We do," said Meredith. "You'd better get dressed. You don't want to be late." Richard looked at her, silently handed her the paper, and turned, the door hanging open behind him. They followed him into the house.

Although from the outside, the townhouse appeared formidably old, the inside was glaringly new. The marble foyer floor swept between towering white walls, displaying small black-and-white photographs, suspended like hyphens. A black Steinway piano huddled beneath the stairs like a spider in the air-conditioned chill.

As Meredith gazed, Richard ascended his stairway. At its base, it was theatrically wide, a waterfall striking the frozen pond of marble below. The taper accentuated its impressive height, an improbable two stories. Apparently, Richard had removed the original second floor to create vast upward space, a feeling of absence and freedom.

As a mother, the first thing Meredith thought was how dangerous this stairway would be for children. She remembered the Sumners' suburban stairway, four steps and a turn and then a few more steps, blocky and thickly carpeted. Children have a habit of falling down stairs, and undoubtedly the Sumners wanted to protect Marie. Gazing up, Meredith imagined little Marie, the chubby, blonde toddler in the photograph, wobbling at the top of Richard's staircase. Then she slipped, her tiny body smacking and twisting and sliding, tumbling nearer and bigger until, when it finally struck the marble floor, it had grown into an adult woman with Marie's face cocked to the side like a broken bird's. Then Richard reappeared at the top.

As he descended, his tasseled loafers made a tapping sound. A brass belt buckle gleamed beneath the silver necktie, the pale blue shirt, the gray jacket, single-breasted and slim, a folded handkerchief emerging from its pocket. His hair, slicked against his scalp, would gradually dry to a silvery mat. He had dressed neatly and rapidly, and he seemed prepared to face her.

But Richard was a man. He could not hide his face behind artfully applied concealer and powder and blush. His eyes shone, glowing moons, from the hollows of a haunted night. He reached out mechanically to take her arm, and Meredith shivered. The police were here somewhere, searching. She could hear them, she was perfectly safe. But she could see no one about. She wondered if, the last time Richard had seen Laura, she had been alive or dead.

"Would you care for some coffee?" he asked, steering her toward the kitchen. "I called my lawyer and cancelled our appointment. I suppose yesterday I was trying to buy some time. I was upset about Laura, and I wasn't thinking clearly. You will recognize my arrogance when I say that I can represent myself at least as well as another lawyer can, and at a fraction of the cost. I will be happy to answer your questions now."

"Are you sure?" Meredith asked, surprised.

"Civil of you to ask. Yes, I am quite sure."

Despite himself, Richard smiled as he offered Meredith Bennett the kitchen chair with its back to the fat slotted oak block from which the handles of his kitchen knives handily protruded. Of course, he thought, he would never do that, slide a sharp carving knife from its wooden sheath and plunge it through the fabric of her cheap suit and down between her shoulder blades. That might buy him a moment's satisfaction, but at a ridiculous price. Besides, he had no personal grudge against the woman, who was simply doing her job with bare adequacy. But Meredith obviously suspected him of Laura's murder, and he could tell that he unnerved her. He felt a twinge of enjoyment at the knowledge that he was, however temporarily, in control.

Laura was indeed present here in his home on Wednesday night, and then she had been murdered. The police had discovered that much, and Richard recognized that it cast him in an awkward light. He needed Meredith to trust him, and he must rely on his many charms to ease his way. He was charming, he thought. He was handsome and intelligent and rich, and he smelled like soap and exotic spices. And he intended to be cooperative and forthright. He hoped that a simple, straightforward conversation with Meredith would appease her and shift suspicion, so that he could go about the business of mourning Laura properly.

He had decided to admit their love affair. It was dangerous, confessing an intimate connection between them with its possibility of a motive for her murder, but he believed that his honesty would payoff. Traces of Laura might be anywhere in the house, a strand of her hair, an overlooked mascara, a dainty button from a silk blouse. The police, currently scanning every forgotten corner of his bedroom, would surely find them. And now, at home and exhausted, he was aware of the increasing possibility that he would slip. He might not be able to control his emotion, and so he had better explain it. They couldn't arrest him for loving a married woman and initially trying to conceal their relationship. Call it what you would, it was not a crime.

"Meredith." Richard sank down in the chair next to hers. She turned to face him, and their knees touched. She drew back. "I have a confession to make," he said. "Laura was more to me than a colleague or a friend. Laura and I were lovers." He savored that word on his lips, redolent of perfume and haste and sweat. "After her divorce, we planned to be married. I have lost the woman I love forever." He paused. He heard his own words, and from the depths of his fear and his swagger, his real loss emerged and startled him again.

"Did Laura come to see you on Wednesday night after you came home from New York?"

"Yes." Despite himself, his throat grabbed, and he had to pause. "Laura arrived without warning around eleven. I hadn't told her that my New York meetings had been cancelled, and that I would be returning early. In her desperation, she must have forgotten that I was supposed to be gone. She and Lewis had had a terrible fight, and she had rushed out. She was frantic."

"Did she say what the fight was about?"

"Yes. She said that it was about us."

"Lewis had found out about your relationship?"

"Yes. He upset her, and she left."

Meredith considered. "But they were already getting divorced, and Laura strikes me -- struck me -- as quite tough, certainly willing to stand up for herself. I think she would have felt that having a relationship with another man was within her rights at this point. I suppose that Lewis might have threatened to use the information against her in the custody hearing, but with Marie missing, I can't believe that Laura, of all people, would have become hysterical. There must have been more, and it must have been serious, to make Laura lose her head and come downtown so late at night."

Richard paused to think. He didn't know how much to tell. But he had revealed the affair, and he could feel that his honesty had worked, that Meredith was beginning to relax, to treat him almost as a coworker helping her piece together the facts of the case. He decided to continue. He remembered that conversation, the last one he was ever to have with Laura, so vividly.

Chapter Eighteen

"Richard, what is going on?"

Laura appeared, windblown and breathless, as if she had sprinted all the way from Winnetka instead of riding passively in a cab. The foundation of her life was crumbling beneath her, and her mind was racing to avoid crashing down with it.

"Lewis knows about us. He says he's always known. He made it sound as if you two had discussed it and made a deal about me years ago, as if you two have been playing with me, like I was some kind of trading card." Laura paused, horrified. "Lewis sold me to you, didn't he, like some prostitute, like a plastic doll. All that I've worked for all my life, the respect that I deserved, the idea that I could actually be my own person -- that was for nothing, it was just a farce. I thought you loved me, I thought you respected me. And what I really don't understand is what you had to give Lewis. Did you give him money? Was it as crass as that? Did you pay him to divorce me?"

Laura stood before Richard now in his memory as she had that night, distraught, exhausted, but always diamond bright. Her love for Richard, her scorn of Lewis, and her sense of her own value had temporarily blinded her during the last two years. But now that she could see their triangular relationship as a business transaction, she could slice through the distorting waves of emotion to the very heart of the matter. What, indeed, had been exchanged for what? Richard admired her. She was incisive even in pain.

"I do love you," he said, to begin. "That is perfectly true, and it will never change. I'm here, and I love you, and I need you. Please, sit down. You're aggravating yourself for nothing."

It had been different at first. Two and a half years ago, they had endured a difficult day and too much wine at dinner, and he had studied her silk blouse and her long, white neck. They had ended in bed together, separating at dawn and meeting at breakfast embarrassed but vibrant. After that night, their business relationship had transformed into a glorious, frustrating flirtation -- the brush of hands, a lingering gaze, her fingertip longingly stroking his cheek. Richard had always respected Laura as a lawyer and a potential power, and soon he realized what a dynamic force they could be at the firm as a united front, a marriage of interests. For him, the game became more serious, the stakes higher.

Then Laura was pregnant, and she gave birth. Richard had assumed that the baby would not matter, that it was simply an inconvenient pet to be stroked and fed and then tossed to the housekeeper in favor of more interesting activities. But he had seriously underestimated Laura's maternal feelings. Although she continued to spend long hours at work and snatches of time with him, she became moody and distracted. Thoughts of the baby consumed her. Richard no longer had her complete attention, and he realized how much he missed it. He missed her. And he was afraid that she might reconcile with Lewis, try again to create the perfect suburban family unit. Then Lewis phoned him.

Other men might have despised a woman presented on a plate in that way. She would have quickly become a weight, a stone which they would wish to cut loose. But Richard had not. Lewis's promise of noninterference, his grant of permission to proceed, did not effect Richard's regard for Laura. Because, although the permission eliminated a practical impediment, Richard realized that, most of all, he still needed Laura's consent to take her. And they both reveled in the game. He loved casting himself as the powerful male involved in an intrigue, struggling to possess the wild, difficult woman who would become submissive and grateful. And Laura adored it. She adored the excitement of sneaking around, and she adored having a handsome, powerful man desire her. Lewis's willing elimination as an obstacle, the bargain between them, must, of course, remain a secret between Lewis and Richard. That was one of Lewis's conditions, and Richard readily agreed. Richard had always known that, if Laura were aware of their agreement, she would reject them both.

Laura refused to sit down. She paced desperately, the foyer, the living room, through the dining room and kitchen. "Richard, I can't take this. Marie is gone, my baby, and now you -- you say you love me, but you treat me like a fool. You've lied to me for so long, both of you. Lewis asked me if you had a key to our house. He was furious." And suddenly her face paled, and she crossed her arms over her stomach as if she were in pain. "Richard," and she paused again, and then slowly, "did you take Marie?" She stopped and stood in front of him, her arms clutching herself.

"Of course not." It was his turn to be angry. "I'm not a criminal. And what could I possibly want with your baby? You're not making sense."

"You knew she was an obstacle between us. Maybe you just wanted her out of the picture, and then, with nothing to keep me with Lewis, I would come to you." She stopped, and her eyes brightened. "Or maybe you're keeping her somewhere, as a gift to me. Is she here in the house, Richard?"

Seemingly possessed, Laura turned and started up the stairs, her speed increasing as she seized the idea that Marie was hidden somewhere in his house, that if she opened a door, moved furniture, looked under beds and on the upper shelves of closets, eventually she would find her baby. It was lunacy, the mad gropings of an injured woman. For, what, indeed, would Richard want with Marie? That had been the whole point of Lewis's proposition.

He followed Laura up the interminable stairway, higher and higher, to the private reaches of his house. He found her in his bedroom, their bedroom, clawing the sheets from the mattress, dumping drawers of neatly folded socks and undershirts, as if he might have bewitched Marie, shrunk her to one-tenth her normal size, and hidden her between layers of underclothes. Richard knew then that he must tell Laura the whole truth, that the misery of knowing could not be worse than what she was suffering. It could not matter to Lewis now. Marie was most likely dead.

"Laura, please stop. I want to explain to you what Lewis meant. It is about Marie." Laura stopped rifling. "But I don't have her. Laura, look at me. You must know in your heart that Marie is my child and not Lewis's."

Laura's eyes shifted. "She could be either one of yours."

Richard felt the slap, and he took it. "Listen to me. Shortly after Marie was born, Lewis called me. He knew that you and I had travelled together nine or ten months before. You had told him at the time -- well, why wouldn't you? -- and he was jealous, and he remembered. And Lewis had known from the moment that you told him you were pregnant that the child could not be his."

"What do you mean?"

"I mean that, years ago, Lewis had been involved in the zero population growth movement. He was young and idealistic, and he had taken it to heart. Before he met you, Lewis had had a vasectomy. He was sterile."

Laura sat on the bed's bare mattress and stared blankly into the mirror over the dresser.

"He said that he had hoped the baby would bring you close to him again, that you would assume the child was his, and the two of you would love it together. He would never have his own child, and this would be the next best thing. It just might work. You could finally make a family. Then, when Marie came, he was completely captivated. He knew that, whatever the biological truth, and whatever happened between you two, Marie must be his daughter. He could feel your relationship deteriorating, and he was haunted by the fear that sooner or later I would try to take Marie away from him, that you and I would marry and raise Marie together, and he would have nothing. He was uncharacteristically brave, and perhaps foolish. One morning he woke up and decided to confront the enemy."

"Lewis called me when Marie was a few months old. He explained the situation, and he asked me to sign a paper relinquishing my parental rights. I was astonished. First of all, while it had occurred to me that Marie might be my child, I had no knowledge that this was so. Second, I had absolutely no interest in raising her, or any child. Trying to wrest Marie from him was the last thing I would have done.

"But I didn't tell him that. He was desperate to keep Marie for himself, and he did have something that I wanted very much. He had you. Your marriage was not strong. If it had been, you would never have slept with me to begin with. Your relationship might disintegrate on its own, and you might cling to me of your own accord. But, since I now had power over Lewis and nothing to lose, I decided to be sure. I told him that I would trade Marie for you. He hesitated only for a moment. And then he agreed."

"We have both stuck to our arrangement. He has not interfered with our affair. In fact, he promised to encourage it, by exhibiting the side of his character that you most despise. I doubt it was much of a hardship for him, and from everything you have said, I believe he has delivered. I, in turn, have stayed clear of your custody case, since my revelation that Marie was not his biological child could seriously impede his claim. Your concerns were also in my thoughts, since the disclosure of our affair might render you, legally, an unfit mother, unable to retain custody of Marie."

"That is the whole truth. I know that it appears that Lewis and I have manipulated you, but I assure you that I was motivated entirely by the deepest love and admiration for you, and that I never intended you any harm. I believe that marrying me represents your one chance for happiness. And I never underestimated your intelligence. Indeed, I believed that you suspected that I was Marie's father, and that if you had thought that that information would work to your advantage in the custody fight, you would have confirmed it. I have told you nothing that you could not, with a little persistence, have discovered yourself. I assumed that, for your own sound reasons, conscious or unconscious, you did not wish to know the truth."

Richard blinked, and Meredith came into focus. He was not sure how long he had been talking or what he had said, but he thought he had told her everything that had played out before him as he had felt Laura once again slipping from his grasp. He looked steadily at Meredith. She was plainly shaken. "What happened next?" she asked quietly.

"You have to realize that Laura is -- was a courageous woman. She did not run away from her enemies, she confronted them. She tried to hit me, but I was able to hold her arms still. The expenditure of energy quieted her somewhat. Finally she told me to let go of her, and I did. She ran back down the stairs and out the front door."

"Where did she go?"

"I don't know. My biggest regret in all of this is that I didn't follow her. I was, of course, quite upset by the whole scene as well. I just mechanically cleaned up the bedroom and waited for her to return. By the time I had finished, Laura was long gone. I am not proud of my reaction. You must know, I have replayed that scene a thousand times in my head since Laura died. If only I had done some little thing differently, perhaps she would be beside me today."

Meredith rose from the kitchen table. She had completely misjudged Lewis Sumner. He pretended to be gentle and honest and high-minded, and, like a fool, she had fallen for his act. According to Richard, Lewis had married Laura without revealing his vasectomy, and he had plotted with her lover behind her back. Meredith knew that Laura had been difficult, and she had no emotional or moral problem with the notion that Richard had manipulated her. Richard gave every appearance of being a schemer. That was his job, and he was good at it and proud of it. And she had no feelings for Richard. The anger, the disappointment, the violence came when the person you cared for, whom you trusted and maybe even loved, betrayed you.

Slowly, Meredith walked past the marble stairway. She turned to her host. "Don't leave town without notifying me. I will try to verify what you have said. I'll be in touch." Like Laura, she walked out the front door.

Chapter Nineteen

Angelica lugged Marie thirteen long blocks from her apartment to the church. Tree roots had lifted ragged fragments of the sidewalk, and some segments had expanded past endurance in the frigid winter months, only to contract in July's sticky heat. Twice jagged cracks tripped Angelica, the baby propelling her forward until her heavy purse counterbalanced her and she breathlessly caught herself.

At the base of the stone stairway, Angelica paused to prepare for the climb to the church door. She shifted Marie to her other hip, and the cloth of her shorts and tee shirt stuck damply to her skin where the child had pressed. She took the first slow steps, and despite her fatigue, she had an immediate sense of upward progress. The child nestled her head on Angelica's shoulder as she continued, gradually, to climb.

At the top, Angelica set Marie on her feet and examined her. She was clean and healthy, rosy with the heat, but content. Angelica had combed her pale hair up off her neck into a rubber band on top of her head, where it curled into a soft bun. She wore a second-hand sun suit, red with white dots like a strawberry, and plastic jelly shoes, iridescent pink with sparkles, that Angelica had bought for a dollar at the dime store. Marie admired their flash as she tapped them against the stone. Dancing between the carved church door and the mountain of stairs, she looked spritelike and vulnerable. Angelica took her hand and tugged the door handle. Gradually, the door heaved open, and they slipped inside.

The church was cool and dark. Clutching the small, moist hand, Angelica stepped cautiously along the tile floor. The Sanctuary loomed before her, its vaulted ceiling and bright stained glass lifting her eye upward, past Marie and the wooden pews and the few scattered worshipers, toward God. She slipped into an empty pew and glanced around. She did not see a priest.

Marie scooted onto the bench next to Angelica and rested her head against its back. Angelica opened her purse and removed a plastic bottle of apple juice and the pink bunny blanket, and she handed them to the child. "Here, Bonita, juice," she said. Eagerly, the child inserted the rubber nipple between her lips and began to suck. "Mama will be right back. You wait here." Tickling her nose with a corner of the blanket, Marie drank. Almost immediately, her eyelids began to flutter.

Angelica slid out of the pew. She walked forward a few feet, and then back toward the spot where her baby sat peacefully drinking and dozing. Angelica eyed the worshippers. Two old women perched near the front, their scarved heads tipped reverently forward. Angelica received a momentary shock when she thought she recognized Marie's grandmother Viola. Perhaps God had placed her here, in His house, to discover her grandchild. Cautiously, Angelica approached the stooped form, but her heart calmed when she realized that this woman was taller and sharper than Viola, she was not Viola at all. Straight across sat a gray-haired man in drab clothes, probably a homeless man who had ducked inside to enjoy the cool. Angelica was wary of him, but the odds that he would notice the baby and steal her were surely quite small. It felt so good to be free, to walk without lugging a thirty-pound burden. She hurried toward the front of the church.

She stopped, and again she looked anxiously back. Although she couldn't see Marie, the adults were still in place, the old ladies' eyes closed, the bum cradling his head in his arms. She rushed down the side aisles, toward the old confessional booths. Perhaps a priest was sitting in one of them, waiting for her to find him and tell him her troubles.

"I am so confused," she would whisper to the faceless screen. "I want to be a mother. But I cannot bear children. Whenever I conceive, I lose them. Three, they are all dead. It is a terrible grief.

"Everyday, for my work, I care for a beautiful baby. I love her like my own child while her mother leaves her without a thought. Her parents, they divorce, they fight over the child, and I don't know what they will do. I am afraid. They cannot take this child away from me. I am her true mother, in her heart and mine.

"So, I came to my baby in the middle of the night. I unlocked the front door, I tiptoed upstairs to her room. The house was quiet, and she was there, sleeping like an angel. I was so frightened. I stood by the open window for a moment, to breathe the fresh air. She was my little girl, but still, I was afraid. I saw the knife the painter had left outside on the window ledge, and I knew it was a sign. They were painting the house, you see. They would sell it and take my baby and move away, far away from me. I lifted the screen, and I took the knife and cut the screen like a thief, and I wiped the knife on my shirt and left it there.

"The house was still quiet, and that gave me courage. I picked up my baby in my arms. She woke up for a moment, and she cried, and then she knew me, and she was happy. She settled back to sleep on my shoulder, and I carried her to the car I had borrowed from my sister. I took nothing, not a stitch of clothes, not a diaper. Except her baby blanket. She had to have that.

"Now the strangest thing has happened. Suddenly, my baby's mother has died. I know she must have died in misery, worrying about her little girl. But I cannot bring her back, and I must think of my baby. Now I am the only mother she has. She needs me. She is only an innocent child. But I have no money, and I am afraid all the time. I have lied to my sister, to get her help, and to so many others. But we love each other. Please help me. What should I do?"

Angelica checked all three confessionals. No one was there. She rounded the church. As she searched, she repeated her confession to herself, and she became more and more upset. She knew what the priest would say. She had done wrong. She had stolen a child, the most precious of all gifts. She had betrayed a trust, she had robbed, and she had lied. The mother died in agony, not knowing if her child was alive or dead, picturing the horrible tortures that could have befallen her. And what about the poor father, who had trusted her and been kind

172

to her, and who was now alone and suffering. He would have done the best thing for his daughter. She should have believed in him.

Angelica returned to her pew. Marie lay on her back, the empty juice bottle and the blanket clutched to her gently rising chest. Angelica's eyes traced Marie's angel face, the poreless, satin cheeks, the pursed pink lips, the long-lashed eyelids, the sweet gold tendrils caressing a face that was a reflection of her mother's. Angelica saw Laura in Marie's face, Laura at peace, the open face of the dead. Laura was Marie's mother, and she would always be Marie's mother. Even her death could not change that basic truth. No matter what Angelica wanted, Marie was not her child. Angelica was the babysitter. She felt a sob deep down in her heart, a terrible, gripping ache.

Angelica bit her lip and shook her head. No, she screamed to herself, no. The truth did not matter. The truth was cruel and unfair and wrong. She and Marie loved each other. They had to be together. She would take Marie and run away, maybe to another city. It would be hard to work, hard to explain her blonde child, but she could do it, she would think of something. Gently, she lifted Marie's chubby arm and removed the bottle. She slid one hand under her back to lift her up, to run away. But as she reached out to encircle Marie, the door of the church burst open, admitting a blast of cold wind, which slashed Angelica and extinguished the votive candles flickering on the Virgin's altar. A bolt of lightening sliced across the stained glass, and then thunder cracked, a tremendous, heaven splitting, "NO!"

Angelica snatched her hands from the sleeping baby, clambered to her feet, and fled alone from God's house into the turmoil He had wrought.

Chapter Twenty

When Carolyn opened her eyes, the sun was streaming through the miniblinds into her already simmering bedroom. She stumbled into her robe and across the hall to Mike's room. The bed was neatly made, and his dirty clothes remained in the doorway where she had dropped them last night.

Well, she had slept late. Mike had probably been awake for hours, showered and dressed and read the paper. She retrieved his damp towel and hung it on the bathroom rack to dry. He was probably in the kitchen, scanning the comics and halfheartedly stirring a bowl of soggy cornflakes. She couldn't blame him for his malaise. They were both exhausted from the strain of the Sumners' problems. Carolyn hated to think ill of the suffering, but it was abominable of Lewis Sumner to foist his difficulties onto his neighbors. And it was Lewis's fault, she was sure of that. She knew from first-hand experience that when a family disintegrated, one need look no further than the man of the house.

Carolyn washed her face, brushed her teeth, and combed her hair. She thought of her own husband Cliff, working too hard, then playing too hard, leaving her to raise Mike alone. Of course, it wasn't his fault he had died. In the end, a microorganism had gotten the best of the great doctor. Maybe God had decided to put things in perspective for him, once and for all.

In the bedroom, Carolyn put on a beige belted dress, pearl earrings, stockings, and her house shoes. She smoothed the bed and hung up her nightgown. She had never been one for lacy lingerie, that sort of nonsense, though Cliff had been interested enough without it in the beginning. Eventually, he just got tired of her, and she wasn't going to play embarrassing games to try to keep him. All those late nights with other women, all those lies. At least she had spared herself the humiliation of confronting him. There were no accusations or tears or scenes, only a dense chill, as she shut off her fondness for him. She applied pink lipstick and blotted her mouth. It was all a long time ago. She could barely see his face anymore.

In the kitchen, Carolyn found no evidence of Mike or his breakfast, no gluey flakes or jam on the tabletop. She felt a prickle of concern, which she tried to stifle. Mike could not have stayed out all night. Other women's sons might do that, go to some bar for a couple of beers and a cheap floozy, but not her Mike. He knew how she would worry. He must have gone out for breakfast. That was it. He had decided he wanted a big breakfast and a change of scene, and he didn't want to wake her up to say goodbye when she was finally getting some rest. It was her fault, for sleeping so late. He would be back soon.

Carolyn tuned the all-news station in on the radio for company. She made coffee for herself and Mike, who would want another cup when he came home. He had always been shy about bothering waitresses. He was a thoughtful boy, not like his father, who had enjoyed booming orders at people and watching them scurry. Carolyn listened to the traffic and weather, sports, and the business report. It was all meaningless lists of numbers, but it was noise. She ate a slice of buttered toast and rinsed her plate.

When the national news came on at ten o'clock, she pulled her apron from the kitchen drawer and opened her cleaning cupboard. Fridays, she washed the kitchen floor. Carolyn lifted the Spic and Span from the wire basket and then crept down the steep basement stairs for her bucket and scrub brush. While she was there, she emptied the water from the dehumidifier and started a load of wash. When she came back up, the local news was on. Just more murder and mayhem, she thought, she'd had enough of that to last a lifetime. She switched it off.

Carolyn worked hard on the floor, scrubbing and rinsing, paying special attention to corners and cracks. When she was done, she was sweaty, but pleased. And the exercise had got her endorphins pumping, and she felt less worried, not that she was worried, of course. She thought she might give her furniture a quick rub, but she had forgotten to remove the furniture polish from the cupboard before she washed herself into the dining room. Maybe if she took her shoes off, she could tiptoe across the wet floor. But then her stockings would be damp, and the floor might not dry properly. Oh well, she thought, live it up, she would risk it. She stepped out of her shoes and then gingerly across the shiny linoleum to her cleaning cupboard.

Carolyn lifted the polish from its basket. Strange, the can felt lighter than she had remembered, almost empty. When Mike came home she would send him right back out for more. Maybe he could pick up something nice for lunch too, some sliced turkey and tomatoes. It was so hot, and he was probably tired of soup.

Carolyn recrossed the floor and put her shoes back on. The wet nylon clinging to the soles of her feet was disconcerting, but it would keep her cool. She shined the dining room table and the china cabinet. They hadn't eaten in the dining room in years, not since Cliff had died, but the furniture must be cared for. She probably had just enough polish left for the coffee table in the living room. She hoped Mike would be home soon. He was throwing off her schedule.

Carolyn entered the living room and stopped. Mike was lying on the living room couch, the good white sofa that they never even sat on for fear of soiling its fabric. He sprawled there on his stomach, his hairy legs jutting out over the cushioned arm. Worst of all, a thick puddle of brown vomit congealed on the couch next to his mouth and drizzled down its expensive edge onto the oriental rug. Contrary to her defense of him, contrary to every good quality she had imagined in his favor, Mike had indeed sneaked out last night. He had gotten drunk and passed out on the good furniture like a common hoodlum.

"Michael Ramsey, wake up this instant," she screamed. "You drunken pig! Look what you've done! You wake up this instant and make yourself decent and clean up the mess you've made!"

But Mike didn't move. Violently, Carolyn grabbed his shoulders and shook them, heaving them forward and back. His head flopped on his neck like a rag doll's. Alarmed, Carolyn replaced him and leaned over to position her face next to his mouth. She could not feel even a whisper of breath. She stood and stepped backward, then turned and rushed to the hall telephone. Trembling, she punched in 911.

Meredith stopped her car in front of the Sumners' house. Through the thin lines of rain, it looked even sadder and more neglected. Her acquaintance with Lewis was like some manic-depressive disease, which had initially elated her and was now slamming her into the ground. And his harm to her paled beside his betrayal of his family, who had slept trustingly in the same house with him every night. Night, when Marie Sumner had disappeared and Laura Sumner was murdered.

Raindrops dripping down Meredith's windshield fractured the flashing red and white lights of an ambulance parked down the street, in front of the Ramseys' house. Soggy neighbors clumped together near the vehicle's open back door.

"Please don't let it be that poor baby's body," Meredith whispered to herself. As she climbed from the car, Lewis stepped out on his front stoop. He smiled sadly, a melancholy welcome to an understanding friend. Her stomach turned.

"Meredith," he said as she approached, and he touched her arm. She pulled away.

"What's going on?" she asked.

"I don't know. I have enough problems of my own."

"Come on, Lewis. Let's step inside. We need to talk."

He held the door for her. "Is everything all right?"

"No, damn it, nothing's right. I just finished a session with Richard Orwell. He told me all about your deal. So, you lied to your wife, and you lied to me. What else have you lied about?"

"I didn't lie."

"I thought you were some noble scholar, dedicated to the search for truth. I expected more from you than hair-splitting about whether you flat-out spun a whopper or simply concealed a material fact. You never told Laura that you had a vasectomy, and you never told either one of us that Marie was not your daughter. It looks to me like you have a history of deception, and you're not fully cooperating with this investigation. And Mister, under the circumstances, that's mighty suspicious."

Lewis hung his head. He looked ashamed. Big deal. Meredith glared at him.

"When I was young - "

"Give me strength," Meredith muttered.

"-- I was idealistic and stupid. I believed that the earth was overcrowded and that each person must take responsibility for it. I went with a friend to a clinic, and we both had vasectomies. We were nineteen years old. I can't believe now that I did it, how stupid I was. Shows what comes of living for the greater good, I guess."

Meredith grimaced. "Cut the crap, Lewis. Just tell me what happened."

"Well. I got older. I met Laura, and I wanted to marry her. She joked about having children, whose eyes they would have, you know the stuff, the romantic fairytales that people spin when they're in love and nothing else is real. I was afraid to tell her. I was afraid she would leave me if she knew the truth, and that if I lost her, I would lose everything. And I kidded myself. Maybe the vasectomy hadn't taken, or maybe I could get it reversed. I just wanted to marry her, that's all. So I did, and before we even got to the kid issue in real life the fairytale part fell away, and we were left with Laura, the tough workaholic lawyer, and Lewis, the weak professorial gnome who couldn't stand up for himself. At least, I think that's what Laura saw.

"When she got pregnant, I hoped that somehow the baby was mine. It was possible, we still made love, had sex, whatever, occasionally. I thought that if we could be a real family, we might find our way back to where we had started. But I was no Pollyanna, I knew what had probably happened. At first I tried to ignore it, to pretend it didn't matter, but the possibility kept gnawing at me, and finally I had to know. I went to the doctor, who assured me that the vasectomy was working beautifully. I knew then that Laura had had an affair, and she was carrying some other man's child. It didn't take me long to realize that that man must be Richard Orwell."

"So you wrote off your wife and decided to keep her baby?"

"No. It wasn't like that. I was upset, but I still hoped that somehow we could pull it off. Laura didn't know for sure that the baby wasn't mine. I was hurt, but I was hopeful. I was willing to overlook the whole thing if it would bring us together again."

"But you weren't realistic."

"No. I couldn't know what it was like to have a baby, the worry and exhaustion and the protective love, which can alienate two parents even in a normal situation. And this was hardly normal. As the tension increased between us, and my love for Marie grew, I began to fear that Laura would leave me for Richard, and they would try to take Marie away from me. I knew I couldn't fight Richard for Laura, I was no match for him, and no match for her if she decided to go. But Marie was just a baby, and she loved me, and we needed each other. She was all I had left.

"My solution was a sad commentary on the state of our marriage. Somehow I trusted Richard, a stranger who had betrayed me, more than I trusted my own wife. With Richard, it was nothing personal. He might be willing to make a straight business arrangement. But I knew that Laura could be spiteful."

"So you went behind Laura's back. You traded Laura's baby for Laura. You lied to her, and you used her. And you lied to me -- you lied to the police. Why didn't you tell me all this right away? You must have known it was important."

"I suppose it's because I am the coward that Laura believed me to be. I knew that I wasn't responsible for Marie's disappearance and at first I couldn't imagine that Richard was. So you see, it wasn't relevant. And I was still afraid that if Marie turned up safe and the truth about her paternity came out in court, I would lose her for good."

"You blew it, Lewis. Because now I can't trust you. As far as I can tell, anyone who could do what you did could have done the rest of it too. Where the hell is Marie, Lewis? And why did you murder your wife?"

The front bell rang. Lewis stood and walked to the door. It opened to Carolyn Ramsey.

"You animal!" she hissed. "You've killed my son!" Her flushed red face poured rain and sweat, and her voice rose from a whisper to a shriek. "It wasn't enough for you to destroy your own family, you had to strip away the last shred of my family too. You're sick, you don't care what your disgusting love affairs do to us, what the neighbors think, how many people you hurt as long as you can satisfy your own selfish needs. You disgust me, acting like you're some big, important doctor, when all you are is a cheap, miserable pervert." Her feverish complexion suddenly drained paper white, her eyes turned up, and she collapsed in a heap on the floor.

Meredith ran to the doorway. Crouching, she placed her hand on Carolyn's chest. "She's breathing, and her heart is beating. I think she just fainted. What was she talking about?"

"I haven't got any idea, I swear it."

"All right, don't just stand there, we've got to help her. If you could just pick her up and carry her over to the couch, I'll get a blanket, and we can cover her up and elevate her feet."

When Meredith returned with the blanket, Lewis was still stooped anxiously over Carolyn's inert form.

"Come on, Lewis. She's not going to bite you."

He looked at Meredith hopelessly, then wedged his hands beneath Carolyn's hips and shoulders, gritted his teeth, and tugged with a great show of groaning and tensing of muscles. Carolyn barely shifted. He glared up at Meredith, who was waiting by the couch.

"Maybe if you help me," he said angrily.

"What do you mean?"

"Look, do you want to completely humiliate me? I mean I can't lift her alone. I'm a professor, not a damned piano mover. I need help."

"She can't weigh more than a hundred twenty-five pounds."

"Meredith, I don't care what she weighs. I can't lift her, and I'm not about to slip a disc straining to make some paranoid woman who has just insulted me more comfortable. Either you help me, or we elevate her feet where she lies, which might be a damned good idea anyway."

Meredith knelt across from Lewis. She grabbed Carolyn's armpits, and he took her legs. "One, two, three, lift," she said. Together, they staggered to their feet, Carolyn swaying barely above the floor. They skittered sideways to the couch and heaved her onto it.

Meredith stood back and watched as Lewis tucked two throw pillows under Carolyn's feet and draped the blanket over her. Despite the distressing circumstances, she felt relief. Because, unless Lewis was exceedingly calculating and a damned good actor, she now had proof that he had not killed his wife. He might not be a prince, but neither was he a murderer.

Meredith looked out the front window. The puddles on the sidewalk lay flat and still. The rain had stopped.

Chapter Twenty-One

The summer storm had passed. Sunlight illuminated washed stained glass and lit the air with a dusty glow. The two old women remained absorbed in prayer, and a few damp teenagers who had dashed giggling into the church to escape the rain peeked out the front doors to see if it was safe to leave. When the dozing baby rolled off the wooden pew and hit the tile floor, her wail woke the homeless man, who covered his ears in annoyance. The two old women joined a soggy clutch massing around the child. One stepped forward and cuddled her, but the howling continued.

"Is the priest here? He'll know what to do."

And this time he did emerge from his basement office, the shrieks having penetrated the stone walls and floor.

"Perhaps her mother has left her here in our care," he said. "I'm afraid I'll have to call the police. Mrs. Ryan, can you mind her until they arrive?"

A Chicago policeman listening to the priest's description of the abandoned girl made the connection. He called Winnetka, and they contacted Detective Field, who happened to be in Chicago just a few miles away, supervising the search of Richard Orwell's townhouse. Now Joe Field stood in the church, and he couldn't believe it. He had memorized her picture, but he had virtually given up hope, especially after her mother turned up dead. But he had been wrong, and now he was holding Marie Sumner in his arms. She was alive and healthy, screaming bloody murder in fact. It was a miracle.

Thirteen blocks away, Angelica cringed on her shabby sofa. She had run all the way home, and her clothes were soaked, and she was shaking. She couldn't hide from God. Marie did not belong to her, she should never have taken her away. So many terrible things had happened. Lewis was a good man, and he was suffering. Poor Mike down the street was being hounded for something that she did. And Laura was dead. All Angelica had wanted was to be with Marie. They loved each other, Marie was her baby. No. Marie was Lewis's and Laura's baby. Angelica's babies were dead.

She shuffled around her small living room picking up Cheerios that Marie had dropped and papers she had crumpled. Angelica didn't know a thing about God's grand plan for the universe, but it was cruel of Him to kill her children, one after another, without even giving them a chance to be born. Angelica was a minute speck, a nothing. What possible difference could it have made to Him to let her have a child? Without Marie, the tiny apartment felt lifeless.

She looked out the window. The rain stopped, and the sun streaked the clean, fresh sky. She lifted the window to a blessing, a cool breeze in her stuffy room.   Perhaps she had finally done the right thing. But Marie was in the church, alone and helpless. Eventually she would wake up and cry for Angelica. She wouldn't understand, she couldn't possibly understand why she had been abandoned in a strange, dark place.

Maybe one of the old women would see Marie. "Oh, what a lovely child, and no one wants her," she would say. "I've always wanted a little girl. God must have left her here for me. I'll take her home and raise her myself." Or the bum might steal her. He would keep her hungry and filthy until he sold her or she died of a disease. Angelica realized that she had made a terrible mistake. She must run back to the church. It had only been a short while, Marie might still be sleeping. Angelica would hurry back and gather up Marie, and she would never leave her alone again.   She ran out the apartment door and down the stairs to the street.

In the priest's basement office, Joe Field sat in a wooden chair with Marie on his lap. An only child and a bachelor, he had no natural ease with children, and perceiving this and his strangeness, Marie had taken an instant dislike to him. But among the female onlookers they had discovered two red lollipops, a chocolate bar, a balloon, and a box of breath mints. As Joe made phone calls and held her tight, Marie grudgingly sucked a lollipop and shook the breath mint container, while clutching her blanket in the crook of her elbow. She was going to have to put up with him, he thought, because there was no way he was letting her out of his sight until he had returned her safely to her father. He hung up the phone.

"I can't tell you how grateful we are that you called us, Father," he said to the priest. "You've made a lot of people very happy today. Now, I don't want to disrupt your operation, but is there someplace the police could interview the people who were here this morning? Somebody might have seen something that could help us identify the person who brought Marie here."

"You can use my office, if you like."

"Thank you, Sir. I'm going to go back upstairs and get this thing rolling." He lifted Marie, stuffed her loot into his pocket, and climbed the stairway to the sanctuary.

Angelica rushed to the church steps. This time she had no Marie to lug, but she had run sporadically for thirteen blocks, and she was panting. She just had to make it up those stairs, and she would grab Marie and run back out. They could sit in the park around the corner and rest once they were safely together again.

Each step was a peculiar height, too low to make much upward progress, but too high and deep to take two at a time. Distrusting her rattled instincts, she watched her feet as they climbed. When she was almost at the top, she sensed someone starting toward her, and she eased to the right to avoid a collision. Then a familiar cry sent a shudder through her heart and froze her to the stair. She looked up to see a tall man in khaki slacks and a sports coat carrying Marie. And Marie was straining towards her, reaching out of the man's arms, her whole body wriggling and stretching to get away from the man and over to Angelica. Marie had dropped a lollipop and a box of candy and even her blanket on the stairs, and she was bursting out of the man's arms towards Angelica and shrieking, "Mama, Mama." Before she could think what to do, whether she should scream or fight the man or run away, the man grabbed Angelica's arm and hauled her up into the church.

The Sumners' doorbell rang. Meredith stood over Carolyn Ramsey, who was blearily blinking her eyes.

"Mr. Summer? I'm Officer Scully. Ms. Bennett said you have Mrs. Ramsey over here?"

"Yes, she's in here. She fainted, but she seems to be recovering."

"Okay if I talk to her?" Scully asked Meredith.

Meredith nodded and retreated to a chair.

"Mrs. Ramsey, I just talked to the hospital, and your son is going to be fine. He needs his stomach pumped, and then you can see him, that is, if you're up to it. Do you happen to know what he had for dinner last night?"

"Soup," Carolyn said wearily. "We always have soup."

"Did you eat it too, Mrs. Ramsey?"

"No. I wasn't very hungry. He's going to be all right, did you say?" She heaved herself up to slouch against the back of the couch.

"Ma'am, what did you put in the soup?"

"Just a few carrots and two cans of minestrone. It's not as good as my own homemade, but it's very nutritious."

Scully walked over to Meredith. He crouched next to her chair and spoke softly. "The kid left a tape in his machine accusing his mother of poisoning him and his father. He said to check the soup in the refrigerator, so we did. It's full of some oily, stinking stuff, enough to make anybody very sick, if not dead. I sent some of it along with the kid, so the hospital lab could analyze it. We checked, and the husband died a few years ago, and now this with the son."

Meredith rose and walked over to Carolyn, who was smoothing her hair. "Well," Carolyn said, "I don't want to stay in this house any longer. I've had my say, and I'm leaving. I'm going to see my son." Unsteadily, she stood up.

Meredith took her arm. "Mrs. Ramsey, what did your husband die of?"

Carolyn flinched and then glared at her as if she were completely demented. "Multiple sclerosis. May I go now?"

"I'll drive you," Meredith said. "You're still a little shaky from your faint, and you're under a lot of strain right now. I don't think you should be driving. I'll make sure you get to Mike all right."

Carolyn looked suspicious, but she seemed to like the idea of a ride. "Thank you," she said.

As Lewis held the door, Meredith turned to him. "I'm going to check on Mike, and then I have one more important stop to make," she said. "I'm sorry about the question I asked you. I just had to be sure."

Lewis frowned. "It's okay," he said.

A white sedan pulled up in front. Joe Field emerged from his car, walked around it, and opened the back door. He reached in and pulled out a small, groggy girl in a strawberry sun suit. Her head bobbed against his shoulder as her sparkly plastic shoes bumped his waist.

"Why, that little thing looks just like Marie Summer," Carolyn remarked, as Lewis gasped and ran down the front walk, and one small fist clutched the pink bunny blanket as the other reached out for her daddy.

*

"Mike?" Carolyn gently stroked her son's brown hair. "How are you feeling?"

He looked terrible. His face was white, he had an ugly red rash on his chin, and his body was leaden. A needle wrapped with adhesive tape poked into a blue vein in his hand, as if he were a juice box and not a living boy. Carolyn could trace the movement of his eyeballs under the thin skin of their lids, marbles rolling under a well-worn sheet.

"I'm alive," he whispered, and she couldn't tell if it was a question or an exclamation or a regret.

Meredith Bennett came closer. She couldn't leave them alone for a decent five minutes, Carolyn thought. "It's Ms. Bennett, Mike," Carolyn said, to warn him.

"What happened to you, Mike?" Meredith asked. Well, Carolyn would like to know that too.

Mike peeked out of slits in his eyelids like a snake. "Did you find my tape?" he whispered.

"The police did," Meredith said. A doctor approached her, and they stepped aside to talk.

Carolyn stroked Mike's hand. Meredith raised her voice. "The soup was flammable? You mean if she heated it up on the stove, it would explode?"

"That's right," said the doctor. "It was full of furniture polish. Rather a crude way to poison someone, and it really would not work in soup. And nobody would eat the stuff by mistake. It reeks, and it would taste revolting. The notion that this woman has been secretly poisoning her family with furniture polish is ludicrous.

"Cliff Ramsey worked here for most of his career. He was diagnosed years ago with multiple sclerosis. The man was a prominent physician, and he travelled all over the country obtaining second and third and fourth opinions, trying to get all the help he could. I believe he felt the beginnings of symptoms, tingles and numbness, long before he lost the use of his legs, and he spent many a night here burning the midnight oil, reading and researching and consulting with people to try to help himself. He wanted desperately to get well, to continue his career and live out his life with his wife and son. As I recall, he was very protective of them, didn't want them to know he was sick until he was quite incapacitated. You can't tell me that all the doctors who worked on his case missed the work of this master poisoner Winnetka housewife. Maybe in French novels, but not on the North Shore. The husband died of a brutal disease, and the son is nuts."

Mike closed his eyes. Carolyn could feel the room spinning, the corners of the sickly yellow walls coming closer, pressing her body into a thin, beige strip. The last thing she saw before she fainted again was herself, a young woman, turning her back on her husband's open arms, then snatching up her little son and squeezing him until he burst.

Chapter Twenty-Two

Angelica had kidnapped Marie. But who had murdered Laura? Meredith drove swiftly south on Lake Shore Drive, past the sparkling lake and serene sailboats, water melting into sky. If Laura had returned home Wednesday night after talking to Richard, and she and Lewis had argued, and Lewis had killed her there, he wouldn't have been strong enough to carry her from the house across the yard to the car, and then from the car a quarter of a mile down the bike path. And if the doctor was right and she had broken her neck falling down the stairs, it couldn't have been the Sumners' short, carpeted flight. The police had found a few of Laura's hairs in Lewis's backseat, but that didn't prove anything. It was her backseat too, and the hairs could have dropped when she was pulling out groceries or unfastening Marie from her car seat.

Joe Field had listened to the most recent of Mike Ramsey's tapes. There were over a hundred total in the black garbage bag, the record of a sick young man's longings and anguished attempts to behave properly. The tapes were explicit and disconcerting. And every one of them dealt with his interest in prepubescent girls. Not one indicated any sexual attraction to a grown woman.

Meredith veered off the Drive at the Michigan Avenue exit, sleek hotels and marble shopping malls. Dodging a row of cabs, she turned west down Oak Street, past small, fancy shops, and then north into the Gold Coast area's swanky homes and quiet streets, old world charm only minutes from downtown for those who could pay the price. Amazingly, there was a parking space in front of Richard Orwell's townhouse. Perhaps it was a sign. She dove into it, locked the car, and hurried to the front door.

Before she could ring, the door opened. Richard loomed before her, his eyes tired, but his posture regal. He looked almost immortal.

"Ah, Meredith. Somehow I sensed your presence. Your colleagues on the police force have just left. It seems they have impounded my car as well. Perhaps you can help me accelerate its return. They will find nothing of consequence there, you know."

He stepped aside and swept his arm toward the inside of his house. Meredith entered, her eye drawn through the hard, white foyer to the enormous staircase. She stopped at its foot. She stared up, on and on, toward the top, and then back at Richard.

"Laura didn't leave that night, did she." It was a statement, not a question.

"Of course she did. She's not here, is she?"

"I don't find this woman's death a laughing matter, and I don't believe that you do either. You loved her."

"I still do. But that's no reason to become melodramatic. Would you like to step into the kitchen?

196

I think we could both use a cold drink," he said. "That's allowed, isn't it?"

Meredith followed Richard through the white living room to the kitchen. Opening the door of the massive refrigerator, he removed a pitcher and a lemon. Then he pulled a long, silver knife from the block on the counter. He turned to her. Inadvertently, she stepped back.

"You might as well know, your colleagues were quite excited when they left. It seems they sprinkled some powder or squirted some chemical about, and they believe they have detected a miniscule blood stain at the foot of the stairs. Somehow, they have managed to remove it and rush it to the lab."

"Is it Laura's blood?"

"That really doesn't matter, Meredith. You see, your concern must be to convict someone for Laura's death. Laura's blood could be coating this house, but a team of smart lawyers would be able to plant enough doubt in one juror's mind to exonerate me. I was framed, you see, something of the sort, or perhaps Laura cut her foot during one of her numerous visits to the man she loved. The criminal justice system is marvelous, carefully crafted to prevent the mistaken incarceration of the innocent at the cost of the liberation of who knows how many of the guilty. That was a decision that our forefathers made, in their infinite wisdom, and I, for one, doff my cap to them. Anyone who can afford a few good lawyers and impressive experts can purchase his freedom through the operation of illusion, paranoia, and doubt.

197

Who knows what reality is, and who cares? If there is any doubt, there is no murderer."

Meredith watched Richard. He had begun to slice the lemon into thin, even rings, its acid juice spreading in a pale pool over the granite counter. He lifted the knife, and a droplet dangled from its blade.

"Are you saying that you killed Laura, but we won't be able to convict you?"

"Now, Meredith. We had a real heart-to-heart this morning, and I told you the truth. I have to admit, I am a bit annoyed at the government's lengthy search of my home and seizure of my car, but still, I thought we were friends. You shouldn't use your keen wit to try to trick me, after all we've been to each other." With a flourish, he deposited the knife on the counter. He poured the cold tea into two glasses and added the lemon. "Pardon my fingers."

"But there is a truth, Richard. You know that. Laura is dead, and someone knows how she died."

"What is truth, what is knowledge? It's a tricky business. You and I have to live in a practical world. The practical world says, if you cannot convict me, I am innocent. You and I must admit the limitations of our abilities to understand the past. People are complicated, relationships don't always make sense, irrational things happen. We cannot always use logic to deduce and reconstruct."

"Don't preach at me, Richard. I know what happened. You told Laura your sordid truth, your arrangement with Lewis. She got angry all right. But she wasn't angry at Lewis. She had given up on him already. He couldn't disappoint her more than he already had. The person who disappointed and infuriated her was the man she loved, for whom she was willing to risk her job and her daughter. She was angry at you. You used and betrayed her, and she couldn't be sure what you felt anymore, whether you really loved her, or whether you just got some kind of sick power trip out of controlling her. Everyone she cared about was gone -- Marie, and now you. Did she attack you? Was it self defense? We know you're not a man who runs around murdering women for fun, Richard. Come down to the station. Maybe we can work something out."

The corners of Richard's mouth turned up, a vacant mask of a grin. "We may never know what really happened that night. All I can add to what I've already told you is that I still see Laura everyday, and I believe I always will. So, you see, she isn't really dead. Not for me."

"Fine. I think you'd better come with me to the police station. You can call your lawyer from there."

"Certainly, Counselor. The wheels of justice must grind wearily in some direction or other."

He turned back to the counter and picked up the knife. Meredith backed slowly towards the living room. "Let's go, Richard," she said evenly. "We might as well get this over with. If you're right, and I'd imagine you usually are, this will amount to an interesting blip in your life, and nothing more. You're strong. You'll survive it. Maybe you can even write a book about it afterwards."

Richard rinsed the knife and placed it on the drain board. He strode past Meredith towards the front door.

"After you," he said, opening the door wide. "You're a perceptive woman, Ms. Bennett. But you shouldn't have come alone to question a murder suspect. What were you thinking? Promise me that next time you'll be more careful." He paused. "By the way, Laura did have a scraped foot one day when she came here. A pedicure injury, I believe. Very risky, pedicures. I'll have to speak to my cleaning lady." He followed her to her car and climbed into the passenger seat.

Richard leaned against the headrest and closed his eyes. He hadn't slept well since Laura died. He couldn't bear his bedroom, the memory of her eyes burning there, crazy with grief and loss, the loss of her daughter, of Richard, of her image of herself. He tried to sleep downstairs on the expensive white sofa, but he tossed helplessly in the airy space. He needed to be swaddled, to be encircled in loving arms. He buried himself in blankets, and he sweated all night. Early in the morning he would abandon the effort. He would climb the interminable stairs to his mausoleum shower and step into the hot spray. Wash away the pain, he prayed, and the water did help while he was in it. He emerged and dried himself and returned to the bedroom. He opened his underwear drawer. She had touched these socks and these undershirts, she had thrown them out of the drawers in her ridiculous hunt for Marie. He had told Meredith Bennett the truth.

Richard lay back, and he allowed the motion of the car to soothe him, to lull him into the world between consciousness and sleep. Shapes danced before his eyes, and a story played out, rational and bizarre, real and fantastic. He had no power over the story, no power to start or stop or change it. It just happened to him, over and over again. Now he was in a car, moving effortlessly, buckled in his seat with Meredith Bennett beside him. Meredith, who wanted to put him in jail, but whose warmth and control somehow made him feel safe. Not loved, never again loved, but, in some weird way, cared for. His head drooped, and the story played.

Laura was in his bedroom. She was tall and willowy, bending repeatedly to hurl his clothes from his drawers to the floor, crouching to peer under the bed, pulling his suits and shoes and sweaters out of his enormous closet. Her tousled dark hair and wide, sparkling eyes made her look sixteen, and he had a wild impulse to seize her and push her onto the floor and make love to her among the silk neckties. He would feel the long limbs shudder and relax, the lazy, vulnerable smile would return, and she would be his again. He reached out his hand and touched her shoulder gently, with a fingertip. She whirled around and slapped him, a vicious, snapping smack across his cheek.

Involuntarily, his left hand hugged his face, but his right hand grabbed her arm. She was frantic, out-of-control, a flailing, kicking harpy, her hair in her face, her body lurching violently, her voice a ragged tear.

"Let go of me, you monster! What have you done with my baby?"

Richard clutched both of her arms. He tried to draw her body close, to wrap her in his embrace like a human straitjacket. She resisted furiously, but he was very strong. They stood in the bedroom, his arms tight around her, her body throbbing and pulling and then, eerily, quiet.

"It's all right, Laura. That's right, settle down. We're going to pull ourselves together, and then we're going downstairs. My car is right out front. I'll drive you back home, and we'll both talk to Lewis. We should have done this a long time ago. You can get some of your things and move in here with me. I'll take care of you. We'll get through all this together. I love you. That's all this is about. I want you here with me."

Richard softened his grip. They walked through the bedroom, and he caught her. She was shivering and unsteady. They stood together at the top of the stairs. "Can you manage?" he asked.

"I don't know," she said. " I feel like I might be sick."

"It's all right. I'll take care of you."

They stood together, at the head of the swooping staircase, the pride of his house, the symbol of his life. He let go of her shoulder with his right arm, and he reached under her, lifting her off her feet and up into his chest. He felt her against him, her breath light, insistent puffs, her hands delicate against his neck. She was barely holding on now. She was drained, at his mercy. He pushed his lips against her throat. He felt like a vampire, triumphant and flushed with the weight of his victim. He started down the stairs.

202

He was walking slowly, feeling for each step carefully with his out-stretched foot. The stairs were slippery, and he tried to keep Laura's weight balanced back. He concentrated on his careful, downward progress. At about the quarter mark, Laura pressed her face into his chest and then tilted her lips upward.

"Richard, what about Marie?"

He wasn't sure what she meant. He still didn't know, he would never know. Was she worried about custody, did she still think he had Marie somewhere in the house, did she simply want assurances that if Marie turned up, they could be a family? But every time he replayed that scene, he responded in the same way.

"Laura, as difficult as it is, I think it's time for you to accept that your daughter Marie is dead."

Richard's left foot rested securely on the stair. But his right foot was lowering slowly to grope for the next one. It was at that moment, two stories above the ground, both their weights balanced on his left foot, that she flew apart.

"You bastard," she screamed. "She's your daughter too, but you never cared about her. You're some unnatural beast. This is all your fault, it's all your fault." She slapped his face again, a harsh, ringing smack. Then she stretched her upper body away from him, over the precipice, and she pushed him back against the stairs with all her strength.

It was a reflex. Even highly intelligent, highly trained people with vast reservoirs of knowledge and intellect eventually succumb to their reflexes. Everyone needs them to breath, to move, for their hearts to beat.

Reflexes are necessary for the survival of the human animal. They are instinctive and inescapable. It was not his fault, and it was the last thing he would have wanted.

He dropped her. His arms flew to the side, his right hand groping for the banister, his left flailing toward the stairs, and somehow he did grab the railing and stop himself from sliding down. But he had released Laura, her head flung back over the column of air, just let her go as if she were a cumbersome sack which simply impeded his own salvation. Or perhaps there was more. Perhaps he was angry. She had slapped him, she had pushed him, she had spurned him again. He wanted her, but all she really cared about was that child who couldn't string two words together, who dribbled and fussed and wet the bed. Time and again, she had rejected him for the child, and now she was doing it again.

He could see her fall, head first, as if she were diving, her legs skewed like a rejected doll. And he could hear her, her startled shriek, her bones smacking the cold stone, on and on, mercilessly impelled by gravity and her own force and the slickness of the stone, down and down, until she slammed against the marble floor and lay twisted and snapped and silent.

She was quite dead. His lover was suddenly, horribly dead, and he had to think. It had been an accident. He should call an ambulance, have her properly looked after. But a small voice in his head told him to wait, to think. Maybe it wasn't an accident. He had been angry. More important, he had every reason to be angry. No one would ever know the truth of what he really felt at that last moment, and it honestly didn't matter. All that mattered was what he might have felt. He might have killed her on purpose.

It all became horribly clear. He had to get her out of the house. If her body were discovered somewhere far away, that would throw the police off the trail. He wouldn't be involved at all. At worst, it would buy him some time. He could calm himself and think. He could not have his lover's dead body discovered in his house.

He had no shower curtain, so he chose a sheet. He spread it out, and he loaded her onto it. He used the tail to wipe the floor, to scrub at the dribble of blood that had flowed from her cracked skull onto the white. It was midnight. His car was in front. He packed her into the trunk like a sack of laundry. Miraculously, no one saw him.

Richard drove to Winnetka, her neighborhood, the scene of the previous crime. He parked near the bike path and carried her into its recesses. The sheet was gone now, vanished somehow. He laid her in the trees, alone on the sharp grass, her legs bare and scratched, her white tee shirt, garish red with her blood, over her small breasts. He stroked her sticky hair, and he kissed her still face, and he left her lying there, and then the sheet appeared again, and he covered her with it.

"Richard, wake up." Meredith Bennett was leaning over him. "We're at the police station. Let's go in. You can call your lawyer."

"Was I asleep?" he asked groggily. He didn't think he had been sleeping. It always seemed so real.

Chapter Twenty-Three

Meredith sat next to Lewis on his living room couch. The windows were open, and a pleasantly warm breeze moved the leaves of the houseplants Lewis had arranged on the windowsill. Meredith felt the gentle fingers of air tickling her neck like an old song. A plastic refrigerator filled with toy food and dishes sat right in the middle of the living room on a new lake-blue rug. As Meredith and Lewis chatted, Marie toddled up to present them with rubber chicken legs and pink frosted plastic doughnuts. From the kitchen Meredith could hear the ping of a spoon hitting the sides of a steel bowl as Lewis's mother Viola mixed tuna salad for supper.

"So, how is Marie doing?" Meredith asked, smiling as the child handed her a plastic tossed salad.

"She's fine during the day. She asks for Mama sometimes, especially when she wakes up from her nap. I really can't understand that. Laura was hardly ever home in the middle of the afternoon. At bedtime, she asks for Mama again, and she cries. That's when Laura used to rock her to sleep. I tried rocking her myself, but she really seems to want her mother. Frankly, it's a revelation to me. I didn't think Marie would miss her much. They spent so little time together."

"Laura was her mother."

"Yes, I suppose she was."

"And how are you?"

"I'm pretty confused. I miss Laura too. I suppose I still loved her, even after all the pain she caused me. I wanted Marie, and I got her, but I didn't want her this way. I feel bad. I even feel sorry for Angelica. I trusted her, and she made my life hell, but I know she wasn't hurting us deliberately. My mother thinks I'm crazy, but I'm paying for her lawyer. It just doesn't seem fair that she should own up to what she did and sit in jail while Richard Orwell runs around free proclaiming his innocence through his pricey hired guns. It's surreal, the way the truth gets bent in these situations."

"The truth has been bent a lot, by any number of people," Meredith said carefully. "I wanted to tell you, the lab report came back on the blood at the bottom of Richard's stairs. It's A positive, the most common type, the same as Laura's and Richard's and about a zillion other people's. We've sent the sample to another lab for DNA testing, and in a few weeks we'll know for sure if it's Laura's blood or not. If it is, that will certainly complicate matters for him. We also found one of her hairs in the trunk of his car, and one of his hairs on her tee shirt. Of course, he admits having been with Laura that night, and he claims that he used to put her coat in his trunk sometimes when they went home together. Richard fought with Laura late on the night of her death, he has no alibi, and he didn't show up for work the next morning. He says he was tired and upset about the scene with Laura. But until that DNA test comes back, we don't even have enough to charge him. If the blood turns out to be hers, we'll take it to trial. Whether we'll win, I don't know. If we had a witness who could place him in Winnetka that night, that would be a huge help. We've sent out a description of his car through the media. I'm just praying that someone will remember it."

"Somebody hanging out near the bike trail after midnight? It hardly seems likely. I think everyone around here has fallen asleep clutching his remote control by ten."

Meredith looked at Lewis, the rumpled yellow sport shirt, the smudged professorial glasses, the receding hairline. He probably fell asleep at ten clutching a book. He seemed as if he would be an easy man to live with, quiet and thoughtful and warm. But he wasn't, not for Laura. For her, he had been passive and selfish, and finally dishonest and cruel.

Yet he single-mindedly loved the small pink bundle who criss-crossed the living room with her gifts of plastic food. Marie couldn't talk, she was incapable of complex thought, she wasn't even his biological child. And she was a heck of a lot of trouble. Meredith knew that from raising her own kids. But Lewis wanted her, he clung to her, the way Marie clung to her blanket. Marie and her unquestioning, nonjudgmental love filled a hole in his life. Richard didn't need her, he didn't want the aggravation. Was he more complete for lacking the need of a child, or was the need an essential human part? Meredith thought the latter, but she had observed ruthlessness in both Richard and Lewis. Lewis had not killed Laura, but his deception had played a part in her death.

Meredith stood. "It's good to see Marie doing so well. I'll keep you posted on developments. Goodbye, Lewis."

"Goodbye, Meredith. Thank you so much for your help." He walked her to the front door. She could feel his eyes on her back as she went to her car. She got in the front seat and drove away for good.

After Meredith left, Lewis went into the kitchen. His mother had set the table for a summer supper, folded paper napkins and quartered tuna sandwiches, carrot sticks and potato chips, and two tall glasses of iced tea with rings of lemon hooked over their rims. Saucers of cooked carrots, cottage cheese, and buttered toast strips sat on the table near Marie's high chair.

"It looks great, Mom. Thank you."

"I put in a load of wash, Dear. Could you run downstairs and put it in the dryer? Then we can eat. I want to hear everything that woman had to say."

"Sure. Watch Marie for me?"

Lewis slid the deadbolt and opened the basement door. He reached his hand around the door frame to flick on the bare light bulb screwed into the ceiling, and then he stepped onto the steep wooden stairway, its unrailed sides completely open to the air. He closed the door carefully behind him and tested the handle to be sure that Marie could not tug it open. The stairs were terribly treacherous, and now that she was getting bigger, he really must call a carpenter to build a couple of banisters.

It wasn't safe for his mother either, and she insisted on going down to do the laundry now that Angelica was gone. He wondered at his mother. He could hardly stand the basement after all that had happened, but she was tough, and that gave him strength.

Barefoot in her suit skirt and blouse, Meredith rinsed her hands at the open kitchen window. She watched her daughters practicing cartwheels on the grass, their thin legs bursting into the air. They looked sunbaked and happy. This was so simple and peaceful, the way family life should be. She was glad she had decided to come home early.

Work, with its usual cast of shoplifters, was more depressing than ever after the excitement of the Sumner case. Her daughters had surprised her, handling the occasional late night with grace. At this point, she probably could take on a little more responsibility, maybe not a full load of felonies, but some variety. She would sound them out at the office tomorrow. She'd certainly paid her dues.

The Sumner case still pricked at her. They had developed a reasonable circumstantial case against Richard Orwell, but she couldn't for the life of her decipher his motive. He seemed to have loved Laura, and he gained nothing through her death, nothing that Meredith could see. No matter what quantity of Laura's blood lay sprinkled about his townhouse, no matter how big a jerk he was and how oddly he had acted around the

210

time of Laura's death, Meredith didn't think a jury of ordinary people using their common sense was going to believe that Richard Orwell, wealthy lawyer and respectable citizen, had killed Laura Sumner unless he had a damn good reason. As an ordinary person using her own common sense, she didn't quite believe it either.

Meredith wandered into the living room and lifted their snack-stained copy of <u>The Complete Fairy Tales of The Brothers Grimm</u> from the coffee table. She brought it out to the picnic table, and Maggie and Lucy scooted in next to her, one on each side. With Lucy's sweat familiarly penetrating her shirt sleeve, Meredith began to read their favorite stories of virtuous children and wicked stepmothers, "Cinderella" and "Hansel and Gretel," "The Six Swans" and "Snow White."

Her mind drifted, and she thought about Alexander and the adorable Shawna. If something happened to Meredith, Maggie and Lucy would wind up with a goofy stepmother. Of course, a full parental dose of Maggie and Lucy might turn Shawna wicked, but Shawna would not be put to the test. Meredith was not some ephemeral fairytale mother about to vanish inexplicably from the earth. And if Shawna and Alexander ever tried to separate her from her daughters, she would fight them. Just as Laura Sumner had fought for Marie.

Although she had felt a fleeting fondness for him, Meredith now knew that Lewis would never have made a good husband for her. He was deceitful, with a reasonableness and practicality that were particularly insidious. And Laura had had a point too.

He was weak. He enjoyed succumbing to the demands of others and then casting himself as a victim. Again, Meredith considered the fairy stories, the passive husbands and fathers, incapable of helping their children escape the stepmothers they had blindly chosen. Lewis might remarry, probably another woman who would, either because of her own character or Lewis's provocation, boss him and humiliate him and make his life an apparent hell. Marie might very well acquire a wicked stepmother.

Except that now Lewis had his mother Viola again. Viola was always around, in the kitchen, in the bathroom, polishing furniture and bathing Marie and whipping up tuna salads. She had been lonely in her apartment with her pathetic kitty-cat, and now that she had regained her son, she would want to keep him. Mothers-in-law were something like wicked stepmothers too, Meredith realized, and Viola had been Laura's. Viola would have been happy if she could have led Laura into the woods and left her there, and Lewis wouldn't have stopped her. Now that Laura was dead, she had resumed her role as the woman of Lewis's house. With at least Lewis's tacit consent, Viola had moved right in and taken Laura's place.

"All done, girls," Meredith said, closing the book. As Maggie and Lucy drowsed in the late afternoon sunshine, Meredith suddenly sat up straight.

Lewis stood transfixed in the basement. He remembered it all so vividly. He had waited for Laura outside Richard's townhouse. He knew that she would run to Richard, and he had come after her, but it was humiliating to sit there in the car, watching the house, wondering if she would emerge. He didn't know if Richard would be able to calm her down, but he didn't think so. She was more upset than he had ever seen her. Richard would try to turn the whole thing around and make it Lewis's fault. Then Laura would come rushing back out, desperate to confront him, when he had done nothing but acquiesce in Richard's scheme. Lewis didn't know why he was waiting for her. He supposed he was drawn to her, like neighbors hovering around a car accident. And he was miserable and overwrought, and he couldn't sleep. And he knew that she would want him. He might as well save her the cab fare.

At midnight, Laura flew out of Richard's front door, as anticipated. She spotted Lewis immediately, as if she still expected, out of long habit, that he would be wherever she wanted him to be whenever she wanted him, and she jumped into the passenger seat. She never questioned his presence.

"Take me home," she said. "I want to pack a few things. I'm moving the hell out."

"Are you moving in with Richard?"

"No. You're both pigs. I'm getting the hell out, that's all."

He had driven her home. It was a long drive, conducted in silence as if he were her chauffeur, but he could feel the heat rising off her. He parked in the garage, and they walked in together, through the back door.

Lewis's mother sat at the kitchen table with an untouched cup of tea. It was a fragile china cup, cream with pink roses, a wedding gift.

Laura froze. "Oh my God, I should have known. What in hell is she doing here?"

"It's late," said Viola. "Nobody answered the phone. Lewis is my son, I was worried about him. But, then, you wouldn't understand that."

Laura flushed. "You miserable bitch. This is still my house. I want you out of here. You're probably responsible for half our troubles, and I don't have to put up with the sight of you. I'm taking one suitcase, Lewis, and I'm going to a hotel. I don't suppose I could blast you out of here with explosives, and I've had all I can take for tonight. I expect you to call me immediately if there is any word about Marie. Anything. You can leave a message on my voice mail. When I come back up, Viola, I expect you to be gone. And leave your key on the kitchen table. I don't want any more surprises."

Laura unlatched the basement door and opened it wide. Lewis knew she was going down for a suitcase, and he wondered if he ought to help her. She stepped down two steps and reached for the light switch. Then she turned.

"Oh, Viola, I almost forgot. I got some news today, and it might interest you almost as much as it did me. Come here for a moment, and I'll let you in on it. I'll have to whisper, because it's of a somewhat personal nature. Of course, you may know already, since you and your son are so close."

"Laura, please," Lewis said, as his mother rose and cautiously approached the glittering, dangerous object.

"This isn't something wives usually discuss with their mothers-in-law. You see, the matter is a little delicate. But I think that any woman in a close relationship with Lewis ought to know the truth about him. And he's certainly not going to volunteer it. You see, his male apparatus -- well, it's not in full working order."

Viola's face turned purple. She took one deep breath, and then another, and she retracted her arms into her chest. Lewis thought she was having a heart attack. Then he saw the arms shoot forward, spotted claws extended, as she rammed Laura with every ounce of her strength.

It was almost comical how easy Laura was to eliminate. She had been so loud and full of herself just a few seconds before. She gasped once, a kind of half scream, as she pitched violently backward. It was a neat, angled fall, no bouncing along the stairs, nothing to grab hold of, just a half-cocked swan dive over the edge and then ten feet down on her head. She lay in a bent heap on the cement to the right of the stairway. Lewis stumbled down to her, his whole body shaking.

I'm sorry, Dear." His mother stood quivering at the top of the stairs. "It just came over me. What she said was so vicious. And I still have the bruises on my arm from where she -- "

"I know, Mother. You don't have to explain."

Lewis stooped down over Laura and gently touched her arm. A thread of blood ran from her mouth onto the floor. He knew that she was dead, but it was hard to take it all in.

"But I'm afraid no one will believe this -- that it was an accident. That Bennett woman -- she knows how I feel and you -- what if they think you did this?"

"But it was an accident, Mother. They'll have to believe the truth."

Lewis stood up, and they gazed into each other's wide eyes, and each knew that the other felt the same mixture of horror and relief .

"They won't understand, Son. They'll accuse you, and then I'll have to tell them what I did." Viola started to sob. "I don't want to die in prison, all by myself. I don't deserve it. I should be with the people I love, in comfort in my old age. She did this to me, she did." Viola pointed a curved finger at Laura. "This is all her fault. Why do I have to pay and pay and pay?"

"It's all right, Mother. I can see what we have to do. Just give me a minute. I need to think, and it's difficult."

Neither one of them could have managed it alone, but they had always worked well together. Lewis sent Viola up to the linen closet for an old sheet. They spread it out next to Laura on the floor.

"I don't want to touch her," Viola whimpered. "She's staring at me so."

"That's all right. I think I can turn her onto this if you'll stand on the corner to hold it still. But you'll have to help with the rest. I'll cover her face."

Lewis put his hands under Laura's hips and shoulders, trying to flip her onto the sheet. At first she only slid, leaving a puddle of blood and then a smear, but finally he turned her onto it. He tugged on the edge of the cloth until she skidded toward the center and then wrapped the sheet completely over her on both sides and twisted the ends, like a chrysalis.

"What about the blood?" Viola asked, pointing to the mess on the floor.

"We'll get it later. Do you want to be the head or the foot?"

"The foot, I guess."

"Okay."

Lewis heaved his end up toward his waist and began to pull. She was heavy, but the sheet created a smooth surface, and together, with some starting and stopping, they were able to drag her up the stairs. They paused in the kitchen to rest. Lewis wiped his sweaty palms on his pants and pushed his glasses up his nose.

"That was the worst of it. I'll be right back."

Lewis went into the backyard. Next to the lilac bush he found Marie's wagon. He removed the plastic pail and shovel and placed them carefully on the grass. Then he pulled the wagon up beside the step outside the kitchen door. Viola had moved the highchair and the doormat, leaving a clear pathway to slide Laura's body to the back step.

"All right, Mother, on a count of three."

They each lifted an end to heave Laura into the wagon. She was tall, and it was awkward, her broken neck dangling off the front end like a snapped rose, and her legs trailing out behind. Lewis tugged, and Viola held the legs off the lawn, and they maneuvered her into the garage. Then Lewis crawled into the back seat of the car and dragged Laura, still wrapped in the sheet, onto the floor. He loaded the wagon into the trunk, and he and his mother got in the front seat. He rested his head on the steering wheel.

"Where are we going?" Viola asked timidly.

He was so nervous and shaky, he could barely remember how to drive. He was afraid to go all the way to the forest preserve. He might get into an accident or run a red light, and he certainly didn't want a chat with the police. There were some woods beside the bicycle path, and it was much closer, and no one would be there at this time of night. He drove to the base of the path in Kenilworth and parked. Together, he and his mother yanked Laura back into the wagon. The path was flat, and it was relatively easy for them to haul her another couple of blocks along it. Moving the wagon through the weeds toward the trees had been more difficult, even with Viola pushing, and he probably gave up sooner than he should have.

Lewis opened the sheet. In the dim glow of the streetlights below, he could see Laura's crystal eyes shining. They rolled her out of the sheet and onto the ground, where she landed face up and staring. He tried desperately to bury her, but he was scratching at the dirt with sticks and his fingers, and the ground was too hard and it was taking too long without the proper tools.

"They'll find her right away, with her gawking like that."

Lewis knew that this was some kind of primitive thinking, that if Laura could see them -- which she couldn't, but her eyes gleamed so brightly she seemed to see everything -- then someone happening by could see her.

"What do you want me to do?"

"Well, I was thinking," said Viola hesitantly. "Why did somebody kill her? There has to be a reason. Why does a maniac kill any woman walking alone in the woods? Couldn't you – "

"Mother!" Lewis stood up.

"I mean, just rumple her clothes or something." She looked at Lewis firmly. "Take off her shirt."

Viola turned her back. Lewis sat beside Laura's head and put his forehead in his hands. A few warm tears squeezed from his eyes and pooled inside his glasses. Finally, he reached down and grasped the bottom of Laura's white cotton tee shirt. Carefully, he pulled it up over her arms and crooked head, like undressing a newborn baby. He reached under her back and unhooked her bra. He slipped the straps from her shoulders and crumpled it in the weeds beside her. Her small white breasts glowed like twin moons. He touched her naked arm. It was soft and cool. He spread the shirt neatly over her face, stood up, and walked away. Viola gathered the sheet into the wagon and pulled it back to the car.

"It'll be all right, Son," she said. "Thank you. You did the right thing."

He and his mother had gone home. He couldn't cope with it anymore, he had gone straight to bed, but Viola had bleached the sheet and scrubbed the floors. When Meredith had arrived to inform him of his wife's death, Viola was still cleaning.

Now, Lewis lifted the lid of the washing machine and moved clods of wet, rung clothes to the dryer. He pushed the button and listened for a moment to the warm flop the clean clothes made as they tumbled around. He looked at the floor where his mother had scrubbed it, where the stairway area was cleaner than the rest. Well, they had several weeks, until those DNA results came back negative, to dirty it up. And who knew, they might get lucky. The blood at Richard's could be Laura's. If not, there were a lot of unsolved murders, even here on the North Shore.

"Lewis, what's taking you so long?"

Lewis stepped back upstairs and bolted the basement door. "All set, Mom." He looked at the neatly laid table, and Marie, shiny clean, in her highchair. "Thanks for taking such good care of us. You've really been an enormous help."

"Don't mention it, Dear. That's what mothers are for. Besides, I've never had so much lovely time alone with my granddaughter. She's such a sweetheart. She looks just like you did at her age."

"Mama," Marie said plaintively.

"That's right, Dear, Grandma. Now eat your supper."

Blankly, Marie picked up a carrot between her small thumb and forefinger and popped it into her mouth.

Meredith clutched the fairytale book. Why hadn't she thought of it before? Lewis didn't have to manage on his own. Even without his wife, he had a mate, someone who would always stand beside him. He had his mother. And Viola didn't have to manage alone either. The minute he was out from under Laura, she had her son. Meredith thought about Viola and Lewis together, about Viola's still capable arm with the bruises on it, the arm she had shown Meredith after Laura had pushed her down. Laura pushed Viola down. An eye for an eye, a push for a push. Whenever Meredith came to the Sumners' house and Laura was gone, Viola was there, in and out of the kitchen. Meredith pictured the kitchen, the back door, the stove, the refrigerator, the sink, the bolted basement door. Viola emerging from the basement the morning of Laura's death.

Who stood to gain by Laura's death? Not Richard. He loved her. If Laura were dead, Lewis would receive all her assets, not just the half from the divorce. And as the main provider for the family, Laura undoubtedly had a hefty life insurance policy as well. And Viola would get her son back, and she would get even with Laura. They both would. They couldn't have done it alone, but together, they might just have been able to manage it.

Meredith ran to the telephone and called Joe Field.

Marie whimpered in her bedroom with the teddy bears swirling above her. In the half-light, they circled around and around, watching her. She sniffed and clutched her pink blanket. Finally, she closed her eyes. Soon, they danced away, leaving her alone in their dark, empty den.

About the Author

Hope Sheffield grew up in Rochester, New York, and then moved to Memphis, Tennessee, where she graduated from high school. She earned a degree in psychology at Harvard College. Although she greatly enjoyed Harvard Law School, her legal career was brief. She and her husband have four adult daughters and a teenage son. The author now lives with her husband and son on Chicago's North Shore. <u>Blood</u> <u>Mother</u> is her first novel.